# A Girl's Guide to Fitness, Beauty, and Confidence

Diana Anderson with Michael Prince

HighWay

A division of Anomalos Publishing House

Crane, Missouri

HighWay

A division of Anomalos Publishing House, Crane 65633

© 2008 by Diana Anderson with Michael Prince

All rights reserved. Published 2008

Printed in the United States of America

08    1


ISBN-10: 0981764363 (paper)


EAN-13: 9780981764368 (paper)


Cover illustration and design by Buddy Blumenshine and Steve Warner


A CIP catalog record for this book is available from the Library of Congress.

# Contents

| | | |
|---|---|---|
| **Introduction** | *Miss U Meets Me!* .......................................... | 3 |
| **Chapter One** | *The Reason* ..................................................... | 9 |
| **Chapter Two** | *Walking the Walk: In Sneakers or Stilettos....* | 19 |
| **Chapter Three** | *Lifestyles of the Fit and Fabulous* .................. | 27 |
| **Chapter Four** | *U Gotta Sweat to Shine* ................................... | 33 |
| **Chapter Five** | *Yes U Can Eat Pizza* ....................................... | 39 |
| **Chapter Six** | *Fit to Be Seen: What to Wear and Why* .......... | 51 |
| **Epilogue** | *Reality Check - The Surprise Difference Between U and Miss Universe* ........................ | 63 |
| **Appendix 1** | *U Can't Eat Pizza All The Time* ..................... | 67 |
| **Appendix 2** | *Exercise Routines Overview* ........................... | 79 |
| | *Exercise Plans* ................................................ | 87 |
| **Appendix 3** | *F.Y.I.'s* ............................................................ | 185 |
| **Glossary** | ....................................................................... | 188 |

# Introduction

# MISS U
# Meets Me!

Hello! I wish I knew your name and where you're from. I wish I could really get to know you, but for now, I'm left to assume a few things about you based on the fact that you're holding a wonderfully uncomplicated and fool-proof guide to get you in shape, rev up your energy, and help you look fantastic!

You're probably a teenager or in your early twenties, and hopefully you read the subtitle and are aware that this is a *girl's* guide. Anyway, now that any males have been humiliated, cried, and thrown this on the floor, it's presumably safe to say that you are a girl ready to change your body in a way that will leave you toned, trim, and extremely proud of your totally fabulous new self. Some of you may want to shed a few pounds, others may want to build and define muscles, some may desire both. Congratulations! Whatever you want, you can do it! If I can do it, you can too. But I'm getting ahead…

Let me introduce myself. My name is Diana Anderson and I'm from

Gresham, Texas, which is like a suburb of a suburb of a small town close to Dallas. Writing stories and watching movies are two of my big loves in life. When I was little, one of the first stories I wrote was based on my

favorite series of movies: "The Teenage Mutant Ninja Turtles." So, being the bright bulb that I am, I figured what career combines the movie *screen*, and writing? Screenwriting of course!

I go to the University of Texas at Austin, home to the 2005 National Football Champions (Hook 'Em Horns!). Anyway, I'm studying screenwriting as a Radio-TV-Film major so I can hopefully do a great service by writing more Ninja Turtle movies. Just kidding. You're probably wondering how a girl obsessed with writing silly stories, and watching guys jump around and eat pizza in green rubber suits got into fitness.

Working out and staying fit is definitely my third love. Let me tell you, I had no idea I'd grow to love working out. But I do, you will too.

I've played three sports every year since the seventh grade: volleyball, basketball, and tennis. And I competed in barrelracing (which is a mighty horseback sport here in the south). I was extremely active, yet still looked like every other girl, even the ones whose daily exercise consisted of walking up and down the mall.

Then, my junior year, something changed. I transferred from a small, private school located in a place even smaller than my hometown, to a giant, 5A high school of 2,000 plus kids. Since I couldn't play all three sports, I decided to play varsity tennis. Common sense dictated that in order for me to dream of competing with this team, I needed to be in better shape. A friend of mine mentioned a gym not far from school where I could "pump some iron" to get my serve up to speed.

I worked out at the gym for about two months before realizing I was getting nowhere. I had not replaced fat with muscle, and my tennis game sure wasn't improving. Despite my best efforts, I didn't look like a toned and athletic person. What was I doing wrong?

My parents empathized with me and sensed my frustration. They agreed to let me try working with a personal trainer to see if he or she could get me out of my rut. Enter Michael Prince. Michael, the owner of the gym, agreed to be my *Knight in shining Under Armour!*

Michael has been a personal trainer since 1996 after serving as a paramedic in the military for four years and earning his nursing degree. As

one of the most knowledgeable and effective trainers in the area, he is passionate about fitness. He's taught me to ignore enticing diet plans and products that leave people feeling confused and frustrated with nothing to show for it. He's also taught me indispensable exercises that have reshaped my body and reformed my lifestyle.

Now, I feel compelled to share what I have learned over recent years with you, a young woman who may be feeling overwhelmed yet eager to build a foundation for fitness without the hullabaloo doled out in magazines and infomercials. Michael and I will present a lifestyle change that is healthy, complete, and balanced.

By the way, when this book uses words such as "cardio threshold" or "FFM," that's trainer-talk, a.k.a., Michael. I steer clear of subjects having to do with anatomy and physiology. Yet I like what they do for me, and I know you will too! Please make use of the glossary in the back to look up unfamiliar terms.

# Chapter One

# THE REASON

What I haven't mentioned yet is the most important, most excitng, and most motivating reason behind this book. So far, this book probably sounds like a fairly ordinary, run-of-the-mill spiel on fitness. But I believe that there is something far greater spurring each one of us toward a healthy lifestyle.

You may have noticed the Bible verse at the beginning of each chapter. As a Christian, I consider them far more than pretty-sounding lines of poetry. These are words I live by, and if you are a Christian, I trust you do too. C.S. Lewis once said the penetrating words,"You don't have a soul. You *are* a soul. You have a body" (emphasis added). I wholeheartedly agree with this. In First Corinthians chapter six verses 19-20, the apostle Paul writes, "Or do you not know that your body is a temple of the Holy Spirit who is in you, whom you have from God, and that you are not your own? For you have been bought with a price: therefore glorify God in your body."

In a world where self-gratification reigns, it is increasingly difficult to lay aside our fleshly desires, worries, fears, insecurities, and vanity and leave them at the cross.  Jesus teaches in Matthew six verse 25 "… not to worry about everyday life — whether you have enough food and drink, or enough clothes to wear.  Isn't life more than food and your body more than clothing?"

As teenage girls and young women living in America, we are constantly bombarded with false ideals and shallow images of what is beautiful and "cool," and surrounded by a culture obsessed with Self.  I'll be the first to admit I have fallen prey to society's traps. My flesh has said to me: *Why don't I look like her? How can I look like her? I'd be happier if I had that or looked like that.*

**FYI:**

In the top 10 most popular magazines, the people on the covers represent 0.03 percent of the population.

For the most part, our culture subscribes to moral relativism where there are no absolutes. The thinking is that everyone should do what is right in their own mind. Eat whatever you want, drink whenever you want, go wherever you want, with whomever you want. It would seem impossible to humble ourselves in somber silence before the Lord and realize that we have let our bodies, our *selves,* become idols in our lives.

And yet when we remind ourselves that our body is a "temple," that we were "bought with a price," and are "not our own," we know that such humility is what God desires. Ephesians 4:22-24 says,"You were taught, with regard to your former life, to put off your old self, which is being corrupted by its deceitful desires; to be made new in the attitude of your minds; and to put on the new self, created to be like God in true righteousness and holiness." When we became Christians, we were created anew. We are no longer slaves to our former sinful bodies. As Paul says in Romans six, we are now "slaves to righteousness."

You're probably wondering by now what all this has to do with fitness, beauty, and confidence. You might even be thinking something like *Well, Diana, isn't exercise and working out a little bit vain? Isn't that all about Self?* That's a reasonable question. After all, major stereotypes surrounding gyms and working out don't exactly scream "Glorifying God!" But I believe that our physical fitness is very important to our Lord; honoring God with our bodies is a call to take care of the Lord's "temples."

Before Christ's death, the inner sanctum of the Holy Temple is where God dwelled. Today, the temple or church is where He is worshipped and praised. It is where the people make their petitions and pray before Him. If our own temples, our bodies, are in poor health–filthy, full of dust, rotting, and unwelcoming–then the Spirit is limited, and worship and prayer become dim. I'm reminded of the Shaun Groves song,"Welcome Home." In it he sings, *"Every closet's filled with clutter, messes yet to be discovered. I'm overwhelmed, I understand, I can't make this place all that You can..."*

God has already made our hearts his home. We have been bought with the precious blood of his Son, Jesus Christ. There is nothing we could ever possibly *do* to repay God for such grace. But as Christians, we have a responsibility to act on our faith. James writes in chapter two verse twenty-six of his self-titled book that "As the body without the spirit is dead, so faith without deeds is dead." If our bodies are lethargic, obese, or malnourished, our deeds suffer as a result. In First Corinthians 9:25, Paul uses the analogy of Olympic athletes to tell of the endurance needed to run the race to "get the prize:" "Everyone who competes in the games goes into strict training. They do it to get a crown that will not last; but we do it to get a crown that will last forever."

We are running this marathon called life for the glory of God, not for the praises and recognition of men. And not only are we athletes, we are also soldiers! Paul exhorts Timothy to "Endure hardship with us like a good soldier of Christ Jesus." We all know what good condition soldiers are required to maintain. And just as a runner for Christ runs for an everlasting crown, the soldier for Christ has a larger task at hand than merely "enduring." Paul goes on to say that "No one serving as a soldier gets involved in civilian affairs—he wants to please his commanding officer" (2nd Timothy 2:2-4).

"Civilian affairs" are what the world pushes in our direction every day through TV shows, movies, the Internet, music, magazines, and advertisements–the "pleasurable" things, the "fun" things, the "if it feels right, do it" things. But a soldier knows that he has someone greater than civilians to answer to. Likewise, we too have *Someone* of ultimate authority overseeing us, and it should be our eternal desire to serve Him.

Being in shape physically helps us spiritually. Let's look at a few examples: It's a proven fact that exercise reduces stress, if not eliminating it completely. Oftentimes, people who fail to exercise wind up with inordinate amounts of stress. Similarly, those whose diets are poor can suffer from innumerable problems–something as benign as chronic fatigue or more serious diseases such as diabetes, heart disease, and osteoporosis. If not properly managed and dealt with, any of those health problems can be debilitating in several ways. Not only can a person be physically incapacitated because of a disorder brought on by a poor diet, but being ill can also cause a person to fall prey to spiritual oppression. Proverbs 18:14 says, "A man's spirit sustains him in weakness, but a crushed spirit who can bear?" When we are ill or weak, there are remedies and cures to uplift us and give us hope. We can rest assured that Christ is faithful to answer our prayers and the prayers of those who love us. Our bodies may be crushed temporarily, but our spirit can still soar. Conversely, there are other times when our *spirit* is what is truly weakened. I speak from experience when I tell you that the *Evil One* knows humans so well that he often uses our physical weakness and ailments to attack us *spiritually*.

A few years ago, I was anorexic. I've never said that aloud or written that before, but it's true. After a breakup with my boyfriend of two years, everything felt as if it was spinning out of control. The only thing I thought I could control was my *self*. I began working out harder than before. I counted every calorie that entered my mouth and punished myself if anything slipped by thoughtlessly. In just a few months, my medium 5'5" frame dropped from a healthy 120 pounds to a frail 99.

**FYI:**

Dieting is a way for individuals to exercise control and can lead to eating disorders. The National Eating Disorders Association reports that 35% of "normal dieters" progress to pathological dieting and that 20-25% of those individuals develop eating disorders.

How Satan attacked me was to suck the joy right out of my life. I didn't know what was happening until I left for college after nearly a year of deprivation and ungodly obsession. During my senior year, I was prideful about my body. I was pleased the day I found that a size 0 skirt hugged my hips or when I saw every rib protrude when I wore a bathing suit. The fact that I was sleeping ten hours a night with hour-long naps during the day, or that I hardly ate in the midst of other people was just a necessary inconvenience to be thin. My passion for God had been replaced with a zeal for my *self.*

The prayers of friends and family, and my willingness to listen to them, got me through one of the toughest times of my life. Going to college opened me up to a whole new, exciting world. My mind was stimulated to search for my purpose and place as a college student. My heart was ignited to reach out to make new friends, find a place of worship, and replace old memories with fresh ones. And my spirit was filled with joy again as God healed me, body and soul.

Fitness is still important to me. While it is a favorite hobby of mine, it's not a top priority and it is no longer about control. It's about my well-being and the state of this house of the Holy Spirit. When I work out and eat right, I know that I am strengthening my body for the work God has planned for it. I know that if I am slothful or neglectful, my body weakens and the invigoration fades.

While working out and good nutrition definitely give us great physical results that can't be attained any other way, we mustn't let ourselves become consumed by them and grow prideful. Proverbs 31:30 reminds us that " Charm is deceptive, and beauty is fleeting; but a woman who fears the Lord is to be praised." If we are to be praised for anything, it should be because we are godly women of good character. Second Corinthians 11:30 says that if we boast, we should "boast of the things that show our weakness." Paul speaks of his own tribulations which include being lashed on five separate occasions, beaten with rods, stoned and shipwrecked. We should "boast" of the things which have humbled us, often nearly destroying us, to make us stronger.

I challenge you to view fitness as more than an avenue to achieve a slimmer waist or toned abs. I encourage you to pray about what God is saying to your spirit this very moment. I believe you have this book for a reason. Maybe you're overweight and have made food an idol that you turn to for comfort. Maybe you're underweight like I was and have been depriving your temple of the nutrients it needs. Maybe you're simply unsure how to even begin lifting weights, yet want to be stronger and feel healthier. Whatever your situation, whatever your need, God is faithful to meet you right where you are.

## Now, let's run to get the prize!

# Chapter Two

# WALKING THE WALK
## (In Sneakers or Stilettos)

*Y*ou might be under the impression that girls are born one of two ways: either genetically predisposed to be thin no matter how badly they eat or how little they work out, or genetically predisposed to be fat no matter how hard they try to eat right and exercise. For those of you who believe that, let us tell you why it's hogwash: There are no perfect bodies!

**Michael:** Bone structure is what you're born with, and that is what gives you the shape to work with. Through diet and exercise, anyone can reshape their shoulders, hips, thighs, and flatten their stomach. Your eating habits and an active, healthy lifestyle will allow you to control and shape the lean muscle (metabolism) around your given frame. Granted, some body types, female or male, are more prone to gaining or maintaining body fat than others. However, that does not mean there isn't a manageable lifestyle, even for those who struggle with weight loss. It can be just as difficult for someone with a high metabolism to gain and maintain a desired weight.

First, you must have the desire and the readiness to make changes. Second, the approach needs to match your goals. It is crucial to keep in mind that you are incorporating a healthy lifestyle as you reach your individual goals. In other words, there is no finish line. Believe me, you will want to continue looking and feeling great!

# FYI:

**The Mayo Clinic has found that strength training:**

- Develops strong bones
- Controls body fat
- Reduces risk of injury
- Boosts stamina
- Improves sense of well being
- Helps us get a better night's sleep

**Diana:** Sure, there are girls out there who have inherited certain tendencies to eat more or carry weight around the mid-section, just as others have inherited traits like larger chests or slender legs. I know a girl who hasn't voluntarily done a sit-up in her life, and yet she has a six-pack. In fact, her whole family combined is a whopping 30-pack. That's genetics. I, on the other hand, only began to see the modest ripples of a six-pack after making that a personal goal. For most women, it's a combination of cardio and core training that gets you sleek, firm abs–not the blessings of DNA. That same girl, however, had to work hard to enhance her calf muscles so she could build up her speed for tennis.  Remember, no one has it all. Like we said, "There are no perfect bodies."

Before moving on, we'll touch briefly on "diet."  What's this rumor I've heard time and again about the frightening "freshman fifteen"–that dreaded fifteen to thirty pounds gained within the first year of college?  Well, the only thirty things you'll be gaining are useful hours of college credit! Stay away from any diet that deprives (negative term!) the body of essential protein, carbs, and/or fats. These are all necessary for a healthy lifestyle. It doesn't matter whether you are trying to gain or lose.

**HOT NEW DIET! NO CARBS! NO FAT!**

The key is to learn how to eat in a way that energizes your daily routines and activities. That doesn't mean you'll never get to enjoy some of your favorite junk foods. But once you put into action a balanced regime for your daily activities, energy levels soar and you'll limit the occasional "cheating." You will also discover that cravings disappear. On the cheat days, energy levels will definitely be lower, which will make you look forward to nourishing your body with the healthier foods.

We've seen the celebrities, some who appear cute and curvaceous, and others sickly and skeletal. The media often glamorizes the "too thin" ones on magazine covers, making them seem to us the embodiments of womanly

**FYI:**

Canadian researcher Gregory Fouts reports that over 75% of the female characters in TV situation comedies are underweight, and only one in twenty are above average in size.

perfection. But beware! Oftentimes they are frighteningly skinny; their frail figures are not to be envied.

Many women pressured under the spotlight make the severe mistake of crash-dieting to shed pounds or exercising excessively without refueling the body with the nutrients and additional calories it needs. As they line up on the red carpet, it isn't hard to pick out the truly healthy glows from the cosmetically-applied ones. ***Fitness is an equal balance between how you eat and exercise.*** Overdoing one while neglecting the other may likely cause unwanted weight gain or unhealthy weight loss. Our goal is to look and feel vivacious and strong, not gaunt and feeble.

It's a given that self-confidence and vitality are important, but that's only part of feeling great. Daily discipline in eating right and working out will not only trim and tone, it will heighten your self-image and make you an overall happier person. Plus it gives you the physical results wanted. Also, ever heard of killing two birds with one stone? Exercising is a way of relieving stress while improving your overall fitness level. You can also kill a third bird once a month because exercising alleviates cramps and improves your mood—not that you're moody or anything. By the way, the endorphin rush at the end is a *positive* factor.

# FYI:

**The Mayo Clinic has found that aerobic activity:**

• Reduces health risks
• Helps manage chronic conditions
• Keeps excess pounds at bay
• Wards off viral illnesses
• Keeps arteries clear
• Strengthens the heart
• Boosts mood
• Increases stamina

Right off the bat (or bench or bike), after I work out, I sense accomplishment in a very tangible way. The sweating, the exertion, the blood pumping…it all contributes to a euphoric state in which you don't know whether to fall to the floor or jump off the walls. It's great!

Another obvious reason for happiness: the whole "taking care of yourself" thing is wonderful. Without getting scientific as to why, when you look good, you feel good about yourself. If you're strong, you feel capable. The fact that you're less prone to sickness and injuries, and more resilient if you get them, is a definite perk. Before I started working out regularly and eating a balanced diet, I would get a cold several times a year and might even come down with the flu. But, I kid you not, since I began toughening up on the outside, my insides have toughened up as well. I've seldom had so much as a sniffle.

*Puh-leeze* don't think that to look a certain way or achieve a certain goal, you need to workout every day and eat right 100% of the time. I'll have you know just last night, my good friend Markquette (who is a personal trainer) and I ate every bite of a chocolate fudge desert with ice cream and didn't run eight miles to burn it off. Personally, I give myself a day of indulgence that includes junk food and complete R&R. Try to limit your indulgences to one

day a week, and if you must have a large mocha latte and chocolate biscotti Monday morning, note that you need to watch what you consume throughout the rest of the day.

As I mentioned, I also allow myself a day of rest without stepping foot in a gym or in a tennis shoe. If I'm on vacation or can't make it to the gym on other days, I make it a point to go for a jog or pop in a *Pilates* tape. I can promise you this: As you consistently discipline yourself to work out and eat right, it will become second nature. Working out and eating right emit a euphoric sense of self. When you abandon them even briefly, you automatically want them back.

Before we begin assessing your goals and changing your life, it's important to realize that it takes time to lose or gain weight, for the triceps to tighten, or for the butt to lift. Patience is a virtue, my dear. Stick with it and don't short yourself by quitting. Fitness, like life, is a journey, and that's what keeps it interesting for me. It's a challenge that never grows old or gets boring. As I embarked upon my own journey and experienced awesome results, I began to enjoy every step. Michael and I promise:

*You will too!*

# Chapter Three

# LIFESTYLES
## of the Fit & Fabulous

What do you want? Less fat? More muscle and strength? More definition? Quickness? Agility? Before you begin your new lifestyle and exercise routine, you need to assess what it is you want to change and go from there. For example, if your goal is to lose twenty pounds, one should focus on persistent cardio multiple times a week and not so much on weight training. Conversely, if you are 5'4" and weigh 115 pounds, cardio could be done just two times a week and weight training three or four times.

**Michael:** Both cardio, and indirectly, weight training burn fat. Your body even uses fat for fuel during sleep, but that doesn't mean you should sleep your day away. Your body is made up of fat, water, and everything else. The "everything else" is given the acronym *FFM* which means fat-free mass. This FFM is like your *metabolism* in that the higher the number, the greater the potential for burning fat for fuel when exercising.

**Diana:** Let's look at the three categories Michael uses to establish guidelines for fitness goals. If you are above thirty percent body fat, your regime should consist mostly of cardio training five to six days a week. If you fall between twenty to thirty percent, then you should concentrate on a balance of both cardio and resistance training. Below twenty percent, then rely mostly on resistance training. If you are less than approximately 14 percent, you need to get your weight up, girl!

To find out your body fat percentage, you can get a skin fold caliber test at a gym with a personal trainer. The Body Composition Analysis/Scale, found at some gyms, also measures body fat by bio-electrical impedance analysis. All you have to do is stand on the machine, type in your height, weight, age, and activity.

**Michael:** So, with resistance (weight) training, your goal is to maintain or increase that FFM so you can stabilize or speed up your fat-burning potential. However, do not freak out on me when that ominous bathroom scale shows an increasing number. Listen up: FFM weighs more than fat!

Now, going back to that fat burning while you sleep concept. If you had an identical twin, and you have an FFM of 110, and she has an FFM of 115, then your twin is going to burn more fat during aerobic training and even during sleep. Your body does most of its repairs during sleep, which is a big part of mental health and staying in shape.

If you specifically want to trim your thighs or de-flab your underarms, there are exercises that will target those areas in particular. It should be emphasized that just because you are content with a particular area of your body, for example your legs, you shouldn't neglect it.

It's best to view your body holistically. The golden ticket is to train it as one, interdependent, interconnected, unit. If your legs are just about how you want them, then enjoy the fact you won't have to spend as much time or effort on them.

Imagine a set of dominoes posed to fall into each other, but somewhere down the line, a domino is missing. Obviously, the reaction is that the domino effect doesn't take place. In other words, it is a much faster process with quicker results when everything works together with no missing pieces. In the Appendix, we give you great exercises, including those that target areas girls often fret over.

**Diana:** My initial goal was to develop a stronger serve for my tennis game and to drop five to eight pounds.  Until seeking professional help, I had no idea what to do and feared becoming "bulky" like a guy if I lifted heavy weights.  I soon realized that lifting heavy is what breaks down and then reshapes muscles, and that there should be structure to how and what you work out. When Michael talked to me about my diet, coached me on cardio, and essentially began kicking my butt, I started to take notice of big differences in the way I felt and performed on and off the tennis court.  I dropped a few pounds, began seeing muscles I never knew I had even in the mirror while brushing my teeth, moved quicker and lasted longer on the tennis court, and overall, felt energized and incredible.

# Chapter Four

# U GOTTA SWEAT
## To Shine

*Y*ou probably don't know where to start. I didn't either. For a not so little while, I thought "rowing" involved an oar and that a "rear delt flye" was some sort of mosquito. Before having a trainer to educate me, I wandered aimlessly around the gym, winding up absolutely nowhere.

I would mosey up to some shiny apparatus that happened to catch my eye, perform a few repetitions, (with *im*proper form!) and move on to the next arbitrary machine. I was afraid to use free weights because I thought those were for meatheads and jocks. When it came to cardio, I would walk or jog slowly beside friends, carrying on conversations, never once breaking a sweat. After weeks of hitting the gym, I saw no improvement in my muscle tone, didn't feel stronger or more energized, and hadn't lost a pound. Michael showed me the light and we're happy to pass it on to you.

The first day Michael trained me, we did a beginner's overall upper body routine. It was amazing. The exercises were tough. I had to learn the correct forms and concentrate on them. Michael had me lift heavier weight than the former sissy stuff and repeat each set multiple times. The rest time between exercises, that I usually spent chatting or dawdling by the water fountain, was cut in half. But the routine was invigorating. I could feel my body getting stronger, tighter, trimmer, firmer with every rep. I remember thinking, *So this is what working out is.* I've been at it ever since.

**FYI:**

Both weight machines and free weights are effective. There is no evidence to suggest that one is superior to the other.

The routines in the Appendix for beginners, intermediates, and advanced are examples of what Michael has had me do since I started training with him. They are challenging, fun, and most of all effective. I promise if you'll commit yourself and do them faithfully, you won't be disappointed.

To supplement the cardio and weight training that you do, there are numerous activities you may not have tried before that are great for shaping your muscles, stretching sore muscles, and burning calories. Keep in mind, if you are lifting weights and doing cardio, these are not necessary. Optional only if you're interested.

Most gyms offer classes such as **Pilates, kick-boxing, circuit-boxing, spinning, aerobics,** and more. Personally, I love spin classes. Spinning involves a stationary bike and an instructor coaching you on how intensely to ride, what tensions to ride against, and encouraging you to push yourself so as to achieve your **cardio threshold.**

**Michael:** Also called the anaerobic or lactic acid threshold, the cardio threshold is simply the point at which you start to feel the deep burning sensation in the area being taxed with exercise. This occurs when the energy needed surpasses the body's ability to supply necessary oxygen. At that point, non-aerobic (without oxygen) metabolism begins. By and large, the anaerobic threshold is where you begin to redline your system.

**Diana:** In one 45-minute spin class, we ride up steep slopes, race along flat roads, and grind through what feels like concrete. It's a great way to get your cardio in, with the support and motivation of others around you.

The point is, there are several advantageous classes to take in addition to the dumbbells, treadmills, and so forth. Even if you don't consider yourself a sports-type gal, I'm sure one of these classes will get you hooked. You might be surprised what you discover about yourself! And if you ever find yourself getting bored from your routine, a kick-boxing class or something like it is sure to jazz things up for you.

There are pictures and instructions for all the 28 exercises you'll be doing–some beginner, some intermediate, some advanced, and some suited for any level (adjustments to weight and reps are made to these). Pay close attention to the correct form so you don't hurt yourself. Remember: Muscle soreness is good, not unbearable aches and pains resulting from improper positioning or too much weight.

# Chapter Five

# YES U CAN
## Eat Pizza

When I began working out in high school, my diet was something like this: Breakfast: waffles with butter and syrup. Snack: sugary "energy" bar. Lunch: Cafeteria food. (Need I say more?) Dinner: whatever mom cooked which was generally not what nutritionists recommend (sorry Mom). And of course, interspersed were cokes (which, here in Texas, are any soft drink), each one containing a whopping eleven teaspoons of sugar.

I figured that since I played sports, I could eat whatever I wanted, whenever I wanted. Surprise, surprise. I figured wrong. While exercising did keep me from becoming overweight, my diet hindered me from looking like an athlete, and actually caused sluggishness and other negatives like brittle nails and bad skin. And I thought it was just puberty!

Let me tell you about a naughty four letter word: D-I-E-T. People associate this word with images of a broccoli spear, apple slice, or tofu square stuck to a diminutive plate. Truth be told, you're already on a diet because a diet consists of all the food that keeps you alive and kicking, whether Big Macs or Lean Cuisine. You can lose weight eating nothing but Snickers in between sips of Dr. Pepper. You just have to expend more calories/energy through exercising or daily activities than you consume. But are you getting the nutrients necessary to establish and maintain a healthy lifestyle and body? So, while Big Macs may keep your taste buds happy, your energy levels will be depressed.

**Michael:** Our bodies are primarily made up of protein and $H_2O$. There are a lot of fad diets out there that leave out either protein or carbohydrates in order to manipulate the body, creating a temporary semblance of achievement. However, what you've done is deprive your body of necessary calories and nutrition in order to lose some water weight and muscle, which is ultimately your fat-burning furnace. When you decrease your fat free mass (FFM), you decrease you calorie-burning potential.

**Diana:** As a college student, I have become well acquainted with three unavoidable things that can plague a  girl's figure and even her grades: cafeteria food (or worse: fast food), busy schedules, and late-night studying. I was prepared, however, with the help of Michael, not to fall into the trap.

The best way to eat is incorporating four to six meals a day.This may sound like a ridiculous idea to you. It did to me at first. But I can say from experience that this regimen is definitely the way to go. Michael always uses the illustration of a fire to explain this principle.

**Michael:**  Imagine you're on a camping trip and it's your job to start a fire and keep it going throughout the day. The initial stack of logs (breakfast) is the most important because without it, there is no source of fuel to ignite the fire. Naturally, the fire will begin to die, emitting less heat (energy). Therefore, every two to three hours more logs will be needed to maintain the flame. Not just any log will do. A huge, sopping wet log will

only diminish the fire further (slowing your metabolism). On the other hand, small, dry logs will keep it ablaze. So in real life, a double-cheeseburger is the sopping wet log that extinguishes your metabolism, whereas a lean choice of meat and a healthy, *complex carbohydrate* is the dry, volatile log that fuels your metabolism.

The typical American views three meals a day as a complete and healthy dietary regime. However, most people leave out breakfast and/or lunch, leaving dinner as the primary meal of the day. Both scenarios are askew of the proper way we should be feeding our bodies on a daily basis.

First of all, as we mentioned in the fire analogy, breakfast is the most important meal of the day. As the word itself implies, breakfast is simply a "breaking of the fast." Upon waking, your body is in a catabolic state, which means it is breaking down lean muscle mass (the good stuff) in the form of amino acids (the building blocks of protein), for energy. In order to reverse the catabolic process, we need to eat a balanced meal consisting of protein and starchy carbs in the morning. Second, if lunch is skipped, or is nothing more than a bag of Doritos, by dinnertime we are famished and will likely consume an unnecessary amount of calories than needed for the vegetative-like state we call sleeping.

**FYI:**

**The Mayo Clinic says that people who eat a healthy breakfast are more likely to:**

• Consume more vitamins and minerals and less fat and cholesterol
• Have better concentration and productivity in the morning
• Have lower cholesterol, which reduces the risk of heart disease

**Diana:** At breakfast, I notice most of the girls (who I commend for "breaking the fast") eating a sugary bowl of Lucky Charms or a billowing blueberry muffin. A few slap grease-laden, cheese-covered eggs onto their plates alongside glistening hash browns. No wonder so many binge later in the day or satisfy their hunger with vending machine rubbish. An example of a complete breakfast, one that I always eat frequently are four egg whites with low-fat cheddar cheese and oatmeal with berries. Michael will explain why this is beneficial.

**Michael:** Food in the morning is always a good thing. Even better, Diana's choice is substantial and healthy. Remember, the body is made primarily of water and protein. Therefore, a steady flow of protein throughout the day is important. In this particular combination, the four egg whites, yielding approximately 16 grams of protein, coupled with about 6 grams of protein from the cheese, is perfect. There's also an extra bonus in the cheese. It's called calcium. Why the oatmeal and berries? The oatmeal helps to replenish your glycogen (stored energy), for the morning activities. This keeps the body from breaking down its own lean muscle mass (metabolism) for energy in a glycogen depleted state. So together, they are a perfect combination to start that fire.

**Diana:** I got stuck with an 8:00 a.m. class every morning my first semester in college. (Thought I'd graduated high school!) So I was sure to have a breakfast hearty enough to wake the dead at 7:30. By 10:00 or 10:30 each day, my tummy would murmur, letting me know it needed a little "log." Before I knew the importance of fueling my metabolism, I would tell it to shut up and wait for lunch. When I did this, my body switched on the "starvation mode" button and I wound up eating exorbitant amounts when lunch time rolled around.

**FYI:**

According to the Mayo Clinic, the benefits of snacks include:

- Binge control
- Extra energy and nutrients
- Satisfaction for small appetites

**Michael:** When you eat breakfast, you've kick-started the metabolic process. Essentially, you have communicated with your body, and have told it, "OK, LET'S GO." Your metabolism is a constant. It never stops. However, it is your choice as to whether or not you want it to go fast or slow. You have to decide what energy source to run on. Do you want to burn fat and carbohydrates for energy (this is the right answer), or break down muscle mass in the form of amino acids? That's why it is important to communicate to your body by making smart food choices.

As I said before, you need a steady flow of protein in order to spare your lean muscle mass.The carbohydrates replenish your glycogen stores and give your metabolism the needed energy for breaking down the protein so your body can repair damaged tissue like muscle, hair, skin, and nails.

**Diana:** Fortunately, as an enlightened co-ed, I packed snacks to munch between classes. These snacks changed daily so I wouldn't get bored, including an apple with string cheese, whole wheat crackers with peanut butter, or a healthy energy bar that was low in sugar and high in protein.

These snacks kept me running from Biology to French to Theater until lunchtime. At my dorm's cafeteria I created a healthy meal for myself from the buffet. I'd reach for a lean protein like grilled chicken or fish. Then, I'd look around for the vegetables, and though hidden between French fries and giant rolls, I chose a baked potato or brown rice along with fiber-filled veggies like broccoli or a small salad. After lunch, it was back on the bike and off to class again.

It's important to remember that we weren't built with an energizer battery attached to our backs. And while we may try to march and beat our drums all day, nonstop, we end up exhausting ourselves. No matter how well you eat, everyone needs a break at some point during the day to let our bodies rest. For me, this delightful part of the day came around 3 o'clock when I'd return to my dorm and take a cat nap for 30 minutes. Even experts like Michael encourage taking some time out.

**Michael:** Taking a short nap not only helps the mind to recoup, but it also allows the body to catch up on lost sleep. This is important because the body does its repairs when resting. In college, girls often get less than the recommended eight hours of sleep per night. This is one way of giving your body time for catch up.

# FYI:

When napping goes longer than half an hour, we fall into deeper stages of sleep which can hinder our ability to fall asleep at night, which is where sleep counts most.

**Diana:** After resting, I knew I'd be going to the gym soon. For a pre-gym snack, I'd have a piece of fruit like a peach or a banana.

**Michael:** Fruit gives you that extra wake-up energy to help get you going before doing something active. Yes, it does have fructose which is sugar, but unless you overeat, it will not communicate to the body to produce excess amounts of insulin, which leaves you sluggish and tired, a condition called hypoglycemic.

The post-workout meal is very important! This is when you need to give the body protein for recovery and repair, as well as carbohydrates for replenishing the glycogen stores. The two most important carbohydrate meals of the day are breakfast and post-workout. This is when your body requires more nutrients so that the metabolic monster does not eat up muscle for energy.

**Diana:** After the gym, it was usually time for dinner, coincidently my most important meal of the day, next to breakfast, because it immediately followed my workout session as Michael said. Dinner was very similar to lunch. It included a starchy carb like carrots, rice, or potatoes since my body needed those carbs, and now Michael wants to interrupt.

**Michael:** Generally, I like to recommend fibrous carbohydrates at dinner because they tend to be lower in calories. Unless your workout is followed by supper, there is really no need to overflow the gas tanks (muscles and liver) with glycogen because they can only hold so much and the excess is shunted into the fat cells.

**Diana:** Okay, back to me. Along with my post-workout carbs, I'd have protein like lean beef, tuna, or chicken. If I had a sweet tooth, and dessert sounded too good to pass up, I'd sidle up to the dessert buffet and snatch the low-cal strawberries topped with whipped cream.

When dinner is relatively early, say between 6:00 and 7:00 and your bedtime is somewhere near the next day, then expect those tummy rumblings to roll around 3-4 hours after supper. As Michael said, your body doesn't need excess carbs in the evening, so a late night snack should be composed mostly of protein. Personally, I keep canned protein shakes in my refrigerator that really squelch the late night hunger that often spurs some girls to crunch on Sun Chips and Kit Kats.

These are all just suggestions that I have applied to my own life and have been successfully able to maintain during college. Michael and I have provided a food guide and one week eating plan in the Appendix.

Before we move on, allow me to plug the importance of iron and calcium in your diet. They are the two major deficiencies of American women for reasons such as menstruation. This deficiency can cause weakness, susceptibility to infection, impaired performance, and the inability to concentrate.

Iron's benefits are too many to enumerate here, but they include delivering oxygen to muscles (great since you'll be hittin' the weights!), improving mental acuity, providing energy, preventing fatigue, and restoring good skin tone. Iron is found in several tasty foods like lean beef and pork, baked beans, soy beans, chicken, fish, iron-fortified cereals, oatmeal, whole wheat bread, raisins, plums, spinach, peas, and asparagus.

**FYI:**

The National Institutes of Health Consensus Conference on Osteoporosis recommends 1200 mg of calcium a day for teenagers and young adults 11-24.

You've seen enough "Got Milk?" ads to know that calcium builds strong bones, thereby preventing bone loss and osteoporosis. Nearly 90 percent of adult bone mass is established by the end of a girl's teen years (that means you!), so it's important to get plenty to prevent increasing bone loss when you're 30. If your body doesn't have enough calcium, you could experience agitation, hyperactivity, irritability, brittle nails, insomnia, nervousness, muscle cramps, depression, stunted growth, numbness and tingling, heart palpitations, and of course, bone loss. Doesn't sound too fun. Calcium shows up in some pretty diverse places: milk (duh), yogurt, cheese, fortified orange juice, salmon, sardines, greens, broccoli, almonds, spinach, tofu, and lima beans. Interestingly enough, weight-lifting actually improves calcium absorption and bone mass.

If you suspect you're not getting enough iron or calcium, consider trying a supplement.

# Chapter Six

# FIT TO BE SEEN:

## What to Wear and Why

While sweaty foreheads, flushed cheeks, less than prom-perfect hair, and beastly b.o. (only kidding on the latter) are givens in the gym, looking frumpy and feeling about as attractive as a cross-eyed platypus are not. There are numerous ways to be comfy, cute, and cool in your workout wear.

It's essential that you choose clothing that is breathable, comfortable, and easy to move around in. Wearing a blousy sorority shirt to run in may seem fine, but big t-shirts often become hot and heavy as you begin to sweat, especially if they're made from 100 percent cotton. Also, if underneath that shirt you're wearing a regular bra, you'll quickly learn your lesson and remember the supportive sports bra next time. More about this in a minute.

Wearing ultra-short shorts

could deter you from comfortably doing an exercise or stretch that involves straddling or inverting yourself, and loose shorts could even be dangerous if snagged in equipment.  Shorts should therefore be a length that is stretch and straddle friendly as well as tight enough to prevent literal hang-ups.  If you are overweight, it's possible that you could experience leg chafing.  If so, I recommend wearing compression or cycling-type shorts underneath another pair of shorts.

A good rule of thumb is to keep ventilated and cool by wearing as little clothing as possible.  Okay, let me rephrase that: Be modest, just don't wear layers and heavy materials that will overheat your body.

You can probably guess what the most important part of your workout wardrobe is.  If you said shoes, congratulations - you're right!  Shoes need to be supportive and specific for the type of exercise you plan on doing. For aerobics, step, kickboxing, and other high impact workouts, you need a shoe that's going to support a lot of lateral movement and high impact activity. Look for an aerobics shoe with good shock absorption and stability and great forefoot cushioning.

For strength training and cardio equipment like treadmills and elliptical, you need a good cross-trainer that's light yet durable and offers moderate cushioning and stability. If you're an athletic girl who likes running and jumping (athletic training), you need a cushiony running shoe that supports explosive plyometric movements, heavy pounding, and stop-start activity. If you enjoy walking, hiking, biking, and other outdoor activities, a hybrid walking shoe with excellent ankle support is your best option.

I'm not suggesting you buy a gazillion pairs of shoes for everything you do.  What I am recommending is that you determine your primary activity and buy the best pair for that activity so your feet don't tire or cause you injury. If you use your workout shoes four-five days a week and rotate between two or three pairs of shoes you can expect to replace shoes every seven months. If you use the same pair daily you need to replace them every four-five months depending on how rough you are on your shoes.

Believe it or not, socks are extremely important. Get the wrong ones and you may experience blisters, friction burns, athlete's foot, and stinky feet. For general fitness, cotton blends do just fine. For high sweat activities like running and aerobics, cool max or acrylic socks are the best. If you hike and walk long distances, a padded sock or wool blend keeps your feet dry, which makes all the difference.

On to bras. Larger breasted gals can carry five pounds per boob! If you are an owner of these awesome assets, you should look for a bra that has adjustable straps for a custom fit and breathable fabrics such as cotton/polyester blends that will minimize chafing. If you're average or smaller-busted, you should opt for sports bras in your size.

Remember, 100 percent cotton can be hot, wet with sweat, and heavy. Performance fabrics that are breathable, moisture-wicking, and quick-drying are the best choices because they don't promote bacteria growth and will keep you cool.

Now for the finishing touches. It's understandable that you want to look good while working out. However, exercising with makeup that you could wear on the cover of *Vogue* will only clog your pores while you sweat, leading to breakouts. Try no makeup and use a terry or cotton headband to keep sweat off your face. If going *au naturale* just ain't your style, then use a tinted moisturizer and lip balm to add color to your face.

And nix the bling. Wearing rings and bracelets will make it hard to grip equipment. Necklaces and earrings will get in the way. Trust me.

Most girls are tempted to wash their hair after a workout. However, washing hair and styling with heat too frequently is damaging, especially to color-treated hair.  I used to believe I would be socially shunned for bad hygiene if I didn't wash my hair after a workout. Okay, maybe not shunned, but I was sure I would break out and look greasy. My stylist told me to resist my fears of becoming an outcast and simply try new ways to style my hair after a workout. Here are some quick tips to help you manage and style your hair *after* you've hit the gym:

**FYI:**

Exercise boosts circulation and the delivery of nutrients to your skin which helps detoxify the body by removing toxins.

For those of you like me with thin, fine hair, try twisting it up off your neck before working out. Wearing a narrow terry cloth band absorbs sweat. Afterwards, blow-dry damp hair at the gym. This ensures that your hair will dry the way you want it to. Then, use a light smoothing gel to manage frizz and control fly-away hairs.

If you have thick, curly hair, pull it back before you work out in a soft, material-covered band to reduce breakage. After your workout, use a round brush and an anti-frizzing gel on dry hair. Rub a few drops of oil through your hair to condition it. Then, use heat followed by cold air to fix any portions that need redoing. Who knew you could go from sweaty to ready without hittin' the showers?

**Here are some DON'Ts:**

Don't use hair spray.

Don't wear tight ponytails. They cause your hairline to recede and your hair to break.

Don't wash your hair after every workout.

Don't go running outside without a hat or spray-in UV protection.

If you've been in a gym or walked in on guys pumping iron in the school weight-room, you've probably noticed that most people wear weight-lifting gloves. You may find these biker-esque things too masculine or downright ugly, but unless you want hands with calluses the size of Kilimanjaro, forgo girlishness just long enough to try a pair. Gloves serve a very important purpose by protecting your fingers from developing rough and unattractive calluses, preventing sore hands, strengthening your grip, and supporting your wrists. They should have ample padding across the upper part of your palm and fit snugly without restricting circulation.

Now that we've gone over the types of clothes you should wear in the gym, let's get down to that whole looking "cute" part. All of us have different shapes. As Michael said, your genetic bone structure can't be altered. So, while we may wish we had longer legs or a shorter torso, we can optimize what we do have by wearing clothes that complement our individual shapes.

There are four basic shapes that identify a body type: the Spoon, the Oval, the Ruler, and the Hourglass. Knowing which best describes your body will help you pick clothes that look and feel great on *you*. Here are brief descriptions of each:

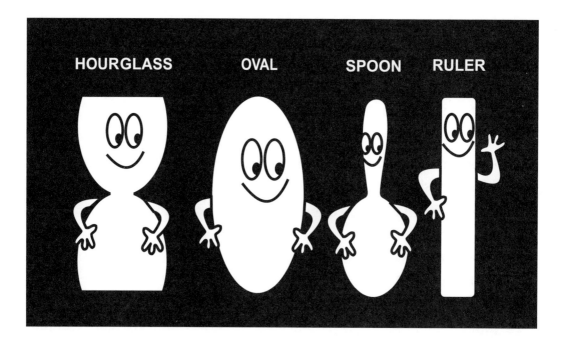

**HOURGLASS**  **OVAL**  **SPOON**  **RULER**

**The Spoon:** tendency to carry extra weight in the lower region of the body, such as the hips, thighs, and butt, while the waist and bust are small. This shape is usually characterized by a slender neck and narrow shoulders.

**The Oval:** usually describes a girl of average height or shorter who is large busted, has thin legs, and gains weight in the midsection. This shape is also characterized by a wider rib cage, round or fuller back, and narrow lower hips.

**The Ruler:** body shape measurements of the chest, waist, and hips are fairly equal. Characterized by an average bust, a large rib cage, undefined waist, flat bottom, and slender legs. Girls with this type are typically lean.

**The Hourglass:** (also known as the "8") are the ideal height and weight for their body. They may have a pronounced bust, defined waist,  curved hips, sometimes protruding buttocks, and shapely legs.

There you have them! While you may be a combination of these categories, one of them best describes you. As for me, I'm a Ruler. I've often been frustrated with my "boy-like" shape because of my lack of noticeable hips, waist, and chest. But discovering how to dress in ways that flatter my shape (or lack thereof) has boosted my confidence especially in gym clothes, which often make a tomboy look like the opposite gender.

Below are some suggestions for what clothes will accentuate your shape.  Feel free to mix and match to fit your unique body, and have fun looking fantastic in the gym!

**Spoons:** You should avoid skin-tight spandex and elastic waistbands as these will only draw attention to the contrast between your small waist and large hips. Pants, such as capris, with a wider, flatter, no cinch waist band give extra room to move and incorporate more room in the thighs and butt with a longer cropped length. Buying them in darker colors like navy or black do a terrific job of elongating and slimming the look of your legs. Wearing solid, deep colored pants with a bright top draw attention away from larger hips. Low rise pants of any length also look great on you.  Tops with deep crew and square necklines balance the look of bigger hips, and don't forget to go bright! For shorts, choose pairs that are lightweight and loose-fitting.

**Ovals:** Since ovals are generally thick-waisted, you should avoid anything that pops out, bulges, or otherwise causes your skin to be exposed. Clingy and tucked in tops are out. And since you're probably slim on the bottom, try black pants with a bright top that has a block of black around your waist to minimize its appearance.

You can wear shorts that are short because you've got slimmer legs. However, don't wear tight shorts as they can highlight the difference between your upper and lower halves.  Tops with a slight flair at the bottom look great on oval types.  Vertical stripes and patterns are flattering as well.  Monochromatic palettes work best to get a taller, leaner look.  V-neck and U-neck shirts also help create a nice visual for bigger-busted gals.  As far as sleeves go, avoid cap sleeves and opt for longer-sleeved t-shirts or tanks. Tops with built-in bras generally don't provide any support. Instead, pair a sports-bra with a high neck or with a V-neck top. This layered look is really cute and not bulky.

**Rulers:** As a Ruler myself, it has always been a mission of mine while in the mall to find clothes that will add dimension to my profile. This is especially hard to do when shopping for workout clothes since there's just not that grand a selection. However, I've discovered surprising ways to counteract my lack of curvature even in the gym.

Generally, any piece of clothing that is tailored with curves and patterns is a keeper. Pants and tops that flair form girlish curves. Soft lines and designs sewn strategically in particular places help create a curvy appearance.  Pants and shorts that are low-rise elongate the torso and give shape to otherwise narrow hips and flat rear-ends (especially those with pockets on the back).  Fabric that is gathered at the sides of shorts or tops easily create curves and add pizzazz to your workout wardrobe. Look for racerback tanks that show off your shoulders and back, aiding in the feminization of your look. If you have broader shoulders like me, stay away from boxy sleeves and horizontal stripes. Try V-necks or tank-tops instead.

**Hourglasses:** Okay all you J-Lo and Halle Berry look-alikes...I feel nothing but envy toward you. Just kidding. While you do possess the most envied of the body types, I'm sure you'd admit to being in need of workout wear advice just as much as the rest of us. Celebrate your curves with fitted or semi-fitted tops. Show off your coveted waistline, girl! Avoid big and baggy, however. This look adds the appearance of bulk and excess weight. Covering your whole neckline with fabric makes your upper body look like a continuous mass. Break up the line of your chest by wearing V-neck tops that draw attention to your face. Also, avoid large patterns and prints as they will make your torso appear wide because of your upper endowments. With a bigger bust, need I remind you how imperative it is to wear a sports bra in the correct size?

For pants, try relaxed fit bottoms rather than those with tapered legs which will embellish the size of your hips and derriere. For shorts, don't wear spandex or cycling shorts unless they are under another pair of loose-fitting shorts because tight, short shorts will exaggerate the width of your hips and any junk that may be stowed in your trunk. I hope you find these fashion do's and don'ts helpful.

*Now in the gym,*

You'll be lookin' good, feelin' great, and pumpin' iron!

# Epilogue

# REALITY CHECK

## The Surprise Difference Between U and Miss Universe

If you haven't figured it out already, the point of this book is not about getting you pageant-ready. Our goal runs much deeper than achieving a perfect bikini body. (However, if you do aspire to be a Miss Universe contender, you might as well dominate the swimsuit competition!)

You see, after a year, pageant queens have to relinquish their crown. No sooner have they cried, waved, and stumbled hysterically across the stage, than they return to being a normal girl, zits and all. Sure, they have wonderful memories and memorabilia to show for their achievement, but they are only one former queen among hundreds before and after them. As for you, your "crown of fitness" will never be removed. It will only continue to shine brighter.

It's an awesome and empowering thing to be a girl who prizes fitness and health in her life. I promise, if you stick with it, your new confidence will be evident to those around you and will rival that of pageant winners and red carpet celebs. Your energy will shoot through the roof. You will feel invigorated and eager to try new things, even study harder. Your increasing strength will surprise and amaze you as your body gets tight and trim. Most importantly, you'll feel comfortable and happy in your own skin as you take care of the miraculous body God gave you

I've had such an incredible time learning about fitness, and I continue to learn something new every day. Join me on the journey that will change your life too.

*See ya at the gym!*

# Appendix 1

# U Can't Eat Pizza All the Time

**Michael:** Depending on what time of day it is and where your workouts fall, keep in mind what your needs are before deciding what foods to eat. Also, your "diet" is by no means limited to these foods. This is simply a guideline to aid you in making healthy choices.

## Making Healthy Choices

| Proteins | Starchy (complex) carbs | Simple carbs | Fibrous carbs |
|---|---|---|---|
| Fish | Brown rice | Bananas | Spinach |
| Beef | Whole wheat bread | Apples | Broccoli |
| Lean Pork | Whole wheat pasta | Watermelon | Carrots |
| Chicken | Potatoes | Berries of any kind | Brussel sprouts |
| Turkey | Oats | Cantaloupe | Beets |
| Veal | Whole grains | Pears | Asparagus |
| Natural peanut butter | Grits | Honeydew melon | Romaine lettuce |
| Low-fat cheese (e.g, cottage cheese) | Cream of wheat | Peaches | Celery |
| Tofu | Corn | Plums | Cauliflower |
| Eggs/egg whites | Beans | Grapes | Yellow squash |
| Nuts (e.g., almonds, walnuts,cashews, peanuts) | Lentils | Oranges | Zucchini |

**Diana:** We've included some sample meals that satisfy and energize. They include the appropriate amounts of protein and carbs necessary for an active lifestyle. Remember, you may need to rearrange the snacks and post-workout meals depending on when you work out.

If you need to lose a few pounds, make sure your calorie intake stays between 1200 and 1700 calories. Do not eat less than 1200 calories. The body responds to the calorie deprivation by protecting fat stores and burning muscle and organ tissue instead. This is the opposite of what you're trying to achieve.

**Michael:** The safest way to lose weight is to aim to lose one pound of fat a week. One pound of fat equals 3,500 calories. So, you can reduce your caloric intake by 500 calories per day or increase calorie expenditure through exercise by 500 calories per day. 500 calories x 7 days = 3500. However, through combining increased energy expenditure and decreased caloric consumption, you will achieve greater results and experience fewer plateaus.

Caloric needs vary for each individual trying to lose weight. I suggest using a simple formula to help keep you within your target calorie zone. Simply multiply your body weight by 10. So, if you weigh 148, you would need to staywithin 1450-1500 calories per day.

# "Eyeballing" Portion Sizes

We don't expect you to have a measuring cup or tablespoon with you each time you eat. Here are some general rules of thumb for you to "eyeball" portion sizes:

**4-6 ounces:** the size of your palm or a deck of cards

**1 cup of rice or pasta:** tennis ball or ice cream scoop

**1 cup salad greens:** size of a baseball

**1/2 cup cooked vegetables:** ice cream scoop

**1 piece of medium-sized fruit:** tennis ball

**1 tbsp peanut butter:** ping pong ball

**1 tsp:** size of a stamp

**1 cup yogurt:** tennis ball or ice cream scoop

**1 ounce cheese:** a pair of dice

# Day 1

| Meal | Carb(s) | Protein |
|------|---------|---------|
| Breakfast | ½ cup quick oatmeal (starchy carb) with 1/3 cup blueberries (simple carb) | 4-5 egg whites |
| Snack 1 | 1 green apple (simple) | 1 tbsp natural peanut butter |
| Lunch | ½ (dry) cup brown rice (starchy), ½ cup broccoli (fibrous) | 4-6 oz chicken without skin |
| Post-workout | ½ cup Fiber One cereal plain (complex) | ½ cup fat-free cottage cheese |
| Dinner | Spinach salad with vinaigrette dressing (fibrous) | 4 oz lean meat |

# Day 2

| Meal | Carb(s) | Protein |
|------|---------|---------|
| Breakfast | 1 cup high fiber cereal (starchy) with 1/2 banana (simple) | 1/2 cup milk over cereal, 4-5 egg whites |
| Snack 1 | 1/2 cup strawberries | 1 cup low-fat yogurt |
| Lunch | 2 slices whole wheat bread (starchy), lettuce (fibrous) 2 tsp mustard, 1 apple (simple), 1 oz. pretzels (starchy) | 3-5 oz turkey on one slice bread reduced-fat cheddar cheese |
| Post-workout | | High protein shake |
| Dinner | 1 cup cooked mixed veggies (fibrous), 1 cup leafy greens salad with 3 tsp vinaigrette dressing (fibrous) | 4-6 oz fish |

# Day 3

| Meal | Carb(s) | Protein |
|------|---------|---------|
| Breakfast | 1 whole wheat tortilla (starchy), 1/4 cup black beans (starchy), 2 tbsp salsa | 4 egg whites with 1 yolk, 1 cup low fat milk |
| Snack 1 | | Nature's Best Perfect RX protein shake made with 2-3 cups water |
| Lunch | 1 small sweet potato (starchy), 1/2 cup grapes (simple) | 4-6 oz chicken without skin |
| Post-workout | 1/3 cup granola (no sugar) | 1 cup low fat yogurt |
| Dinner | 8-10 spears grilled asparagus (fibrous) | 4-6 oz grilled salmon |

# Day 4

| Meal | Carb(s) | Protein |
|------|---------|---------|
| Breakfast | | Nature's Best Perfect RX protein shake made with 2-3 cups water |
| Snack 1 | 1/2 cup raisins | 1/2 cup fat-free cottage cheese |
| Lunch | 2 whole wheat slices of bread (starchy), tomatoes, baby spinach, and 2 tsp dijon mustard (fibrous) | 4 oz low-sodium deli turkey |
| Post-workout | 1/2 banana (simple) | Whey protein drink (25 grams protein) |
| Dinner | 1/2 - 2/3 cup sautéed mushrooms (fibrous) | 4-6 oz lean beef |

# Day 5

| Meal | Carb(s) | Protein |
|------|---------|---------|
| Breakfast | 1/3 cup diced mushrooms (fibrous), 1/3 cup diced red bell peppers (fibrous), 2 tbsp salsa, 1 instant bag of grits sweetened with Xylitol, or Stevia | 5 egg-white omelet |
| Snack 1 | 12-15 purple seedless grapes | 1/2 cup fat free cottage cheese |
| Lunch | 3/4 cup whole wheat pasta (starch), 2 tbsp fat-free zesty tomato marinara | 6-8 jumbo shrimp |
| Post-workout | ½ cup fresh strawberries | Vanilla whey protein shake (25 oz protein) |
| Dinner | 2 cups salad greens with spinach (fibrous) 2-3 tbsp fat-free Italian dressing | 4-6 oz diced chicken breast |

# Day 6

| Meal | Carb(s) | Protein |
|------|---------|---------|
| Breakfast | 1 whole wheat waffle with dietetic syrup (no sugar) (starchy), 1/4 cup strawberries | 4-5 egg whites with 1 yolk |
| Snack 1 | 1/4 cup Fiber One cereal | 1 cup yogurt |
| Lunch | Whole wheat buns (starchy), sliced tomato, onions, lettuce (fibrous), 2 tsp mustard | 4 oz buffalo burger, 1-2 slices of fat free cheese |
| Post-workout | ½ cup fresh strawberries | Nature's Best Perfect RX chocolate protein shake |
| Dinner | ½ cup (dry) brown rice (starchy), 1 cup steamed spinach (fibrous) | 4 oz tuna steak |

**Diana:** I'm sure you've heard the theory about water. Apparently the stuff's good for you. Allow Michael to reiterate the theory to you as a reminder of its many benefits.

**Michael:** Two-thirds of your body weight is water. Water plays a big role in keeping your muscles and skin toned, transporting oxygen and nutrients to cells, eliminating toxins and wastes from the body, regulating body temperature, even assisting in weight loss. That's a lot of reasons to drink it.

If you don't get enough water, you'll become **dehydrated.** Dehydration leads to excess body fat, poor muscle tone, increased toxicity, decreased organ function and digestive efficiency, joint and muscle soreness, as well as water retention.

Drinking half your body weight in ounces of water is a good way to ensure you're getting the proper amounts.

# Cheat Day! (Amen!)
**Michael:** Enjoy! But don't overdo it.

# Appendix 2

# ROUTINES

**Warm Up:** It's advisable to warm up for 6-10 minutes before each routine. A warm up ensures your core temperature is elevated enough to facilitate the safe movement of your muscles during the exercises.

After each routine, we encourage you to do the amount of cardio we suggest. This post-workout cardio time takes advantage of being on the verge of the aerobic zone, and you jump into burning fat much quicker.

**# - This means use a weight at which the last 2-3 reps are really tough**

**Self - This means you should not use any weight when performing this exercise. Your own body weight is sufficient.**

# Beginner Routines

You should perform these beginner routines for two to four months. Two to four months is generally how long it takes for one to move from beginner level to intermediate. Four months is enough time for your body to adapt before moving on to more advanced routines.

# Upper Body

| Exercise | Sets | Reps | Lbs |
|---|---|---|---|
| Side delt raises | 2-3 | 12-15 | 5-8 lbs |
| Inclined push-ups | 2-3 | 12-15 | Self |
| Dumbbell rows | 2-3 | 12-15 | # |
| Overhead dumbbell presses | 2-3 | 12-15 | # |
| Close reverse pull-downs | 2-3 | 12-15 | # |
| Crunches | 2-3 | 15-20 | Self |

After this routine, do 15-20 minutes of light cardio of any kind, keeping your heart rate between 115 and 130.

# Lower Body

| Exercise | Sets | Reps | Lbs |
|---|---|---|---|
| Leg extension | 2-3 | 12-15 | # |
| Stationary lunge | 2-3 | 10-12 each leg | Self |
| Lying hamstring curl | 2-3 | 10-12 | # |
| Standing calf raise | 2-3 | 15-20 | # |

After this routine, do 15-20 minutes of light cardio of any kind, keeping your heart rate between 115 and 130.

# Cardio

Add three days of cardio, maintaining a heart rate of 115-130 for 30-40 minutes on the days you are not strength training. This can be any kind of cardio. Choose something you enjoy the most. If you're not a jogger, try the stationary bike, StepMill, or elliptical. I never thought I'd like running on a treadmill, however, I gave it a week and really grew to enjoy it. As your endurance builds, you'll find yourself actually looking forward to your cardio sessions. And you'll feel great afterwards.

# Intermediate Routines

You should perform these routines for 5-10 months, which is the time it generally takes until you are ready to graduate to the advanced level.

## Monday-Overall Upper Body

| Exercise | Sets | Reps | Lbs |
|---|---|---|---|
| Side delt raises | 3-4 | 12-15 | # |
| Dumbbell Presses | 3-4 | 12-15 | # |
| Wide grip pull-downs | 3-4 | 12-15 | # |
| Incline dumbbell flyes | 3-4 | 15-20 | Self |
| Knee-ups | 3-4 | 15-20 | Self |

Do 20 minutes of light to medium cardio, maintaining a heart rate between 120 and 130.

## Tuesday-Interval Cardio
### (lasts from 25-30 minutes)

Warm up for 6-8 minutes on any machine. Get your heart rate up to somewhere between 120 and 130. Increase speed and/or resistance and maintain for 45 seconds to one minute. The better shape you're in, the longer this time frame will be. Slow down and let your heart rate recover in the 120-130 "aerobic/fat-burning" zone. This should take anywhere from 1.5 to two minutes depending on your fitness level. In other words, it will take longer for the heart rate of a beginner to recover (bring their heart rate down), than for someone who is better conditioned. Depending on your level of fitness, repeat this 5-9 times. Cool down for 3-5 minutes.

# Wednesday-Lower Body

| Exercise | Sets | Reps | Lbs |
|---|---|---|---|
| Alternating walking lunges | 3-4 | 12-15 each leg | # |
| Leg press (feet 10-12 inches apart) | 3-4 | 12-15 | # |
| Dumbbell plie squats | 3-4 | 12-15 | # |
| Dumbbell stiff-legged | 3-4 | 12-15 | # |
| Standing calf raises | 3-4 | 12-15 | # |

Do 20 minutes of light to medium cardio, keeping your heart rate between 120 and 130.

**Thursday- Interval Cardio**  Repeat Tuesday's interval workout.

# Friday-Overall Upper Body

| Exercise | Sets | Reps | Lbs |
|---|---|---|---|
| Dumbbell rear delt flyes | 3-4 | 12-15 | # |
| Incline dumbbell presses | 3-4 | 12-15 | # |
| Cable rows | 3-4 | 12-15 | # |
| Overhead dumbbell presses | 3-4 | 12-15 | # |
| Inclined push-ups | 3-4 | 12-15 | Self |
| Crunches | 3-4 | 20-30 | Self |

Do 20 minutes of light to medium cardio, keeping your heart rate between 120 and 130.

# Advanced Routines

You should perform these routines for 5-10 months, at which time you'll be able to add more weight and repetitions and learn new exercises!

## Monday - Chest and Triceps

| Exercise | Sets | Reps | Lbs |
|---|---|---|---|
| Incline dumbbell presses | 4-5 | 12-15 | # |
| Regular push-ups | 5 or more | 10-12 | Self |
| Bench dips | 3-4 | 12-15 | Self |
| Overhead tricep extension with cable | 3 | 15 | # |
| Tricep pressdown | 3-4 | 12-15 | # |

Do 20 minutes of light to medium cardio, keeping your heart rate between 120 and 130.

## Tuesday- Cardio

Warm up for 6-8 minutes on any machine.Get your heart rate up to somewhere between 120 and 130. Increase speed and/or resistance and maintain for 45 seconds to 1 minute. The better shape you're in, the longer this time frame will be.  Slow down and let your heart rate recover in the 120-130 "aerobic/fat-burning" zone. This should take anywhere from 1.5 to 2 minutes depending on your fitness level.  In other words, it will take longer for the heart rate of a beginner to recover (bring their heart rate down) than for someone who is better conditioned. Depending on your level of fitness, repeat this 5-9 times. Cool down for 3-5 minutes.

**Note: Cardio** This routine is the same format as the one given for beginners, however your anaerobic threshold is going to be higher than it was in the beginner phase. You can do the same program on any piece of cardio equipment.

# Wednesday - Legs

| Exercise | Sets | Reps | Lbs |
|---|---|---|---|
| Barbell squat | 4-5 | 12-15 | # |
| Leg press | 3-4 | 12-15 | # |
| Walking lunges with dumbbells | 2-3 | 12-15 | # |
| Lying hamstring curls | 2-3 | 12-15 | # |

Do 20 minutes of cardio *on the treadmill,* keeping your heart rate between 120 and 145. We emphasize that you use the treadmill because if you use another piece of equipment, chances are, you'll remain in an **anaerobic state.** This can be described as that familiar burning sensation in your legs when lifting weights. Using the treadmill for your post-legs cardio, it's much easier to stay within your fat-burning heart rate zone without jumping back into anaerobic metabolism, which is the phase the body is in during weight training.

# Thursday- Cardio
Repeat Tuesday's interval routine.

## Friday-Back/Biceps

Before this routine, it's important to warm up with three sets of dumbbell rear delt flyes. These warm up the necessary muscles in order to perform a full back routine.  They decrease the risk of injury. Do 15-20 reps with a lighter than normal weight.

# Friday-Back/Biceps

| Exercise | Sets | Reps | Lbs |
|---|---|---|---|
| Close reverse grip pull downs | 4-5 | 12-15 | # |
| Dumbbell or barbell row | 3-4 | 12-15 | # |
| Wide grip pull downs | 3 | 12-15 | # |
| Alternating dumbbell curls | 3 | 15-20 | # |

Do 20 minutes of cardio, maintaining your heart rate between 120 and 145

Ready Set.....Lift!

# Exercise Plans

# Notes

## Beginner-Upper Body

| Exercise | Sets | Reps | Lbs |
|---|---|---|---|
| Side Delt Raises | 2-3 | 12-15 | 5-8 lbs |
| Inclined Push-Ups | 2-3 | 12-15 | Self |
| Dumbbell Rows | 2-3 | 12-15 | # |
| Overhead Dumbbell Presses | 2-3 | 12-15 | # |
| Close reverse Pull-Downs | 2-3 | 12-15 | # |
| Crunches | 2-3 | 15-20 | Self |

# Side Delt Raises
## shoulders

a.  Starting position: arms at the side, elbows slightly bent, palms facing the hips. Your feet are close together, knees slightly bent, back straight.

b.  Raise arms laterally without bending your elbow until it is level with the shoulders.

c.  Return to starting position and repeat.

| Beginner-Upper Body | | | |
|---|---|---|---|
| **Exercise** | **Sets** | **Reps** | **Lbs** |
| Side Delt Raises | 2-3 | 12-15 | 5-8 lbs |
| | | | |
| | | | |
| | | | |
| | | | |
| | | | |

# Inclined Push-Up
## chest, triceps, core muscles
### (identical to a floor push-up)

a. Place hands wider than shoulder-distance apart.

b. Adjust feet so that when u lower your upper body toward the bar, the mid-line of your chest touches the bar.

c. Keep elbows in line with the wrists.

d. Incorrect form is bringing your neck or clavicle toward the bar instead of your chest.

| Beginner-Upper Body | | | |
| --- | --- | --- | --- |
| Exercise | Sets | Reps | Lbs |
| Inclined Push-Ups | 2-3 | 12-15 | Self |
| | | | |
| | | | |
| | | | |
| | | | |
| | | | |

# Dumbbell Rows
# back and biceps

a. Place non-working hand and knee on the bench for support.

b. Hold dumbbell with palm facing in

c. Maintain a stable position with upper body (do not rock or twist)

d. Inhale as u pull dumbbell toward waist, concentrating on getting the elbow behind the body

**NOTE:** I know this sounds funny, but concentrate on pulling with the elbow. This helps you get a better contraction in the targeted muscles in the back.

| Exercise | Sets | Reps | Lbs |
|---|---|---|---|
| Dumbbell Rows | 2-3 | 12-15 | # |
| | | | |
| | | | |
| | | | |
| | | | |
| | | | |

# Overhead Dumbbell Presses
# shoulders and triceps

a. Sit on utility bench.

b. Lift dumbbells with palms facing forward, level with your ears.

c. Keeping elbows in line beneath the wrist, press dumbbells overhead, bringing them together at the top of the range of motion.

d. As u bring them back down, stop at either ear level, or at a 90 degree angle at the elbow.

Note: This movement can also be performed with palms facing inward. This hits more of the front of your shoulder.

| Beginner-Upper Body | | | |
|---|---|---|---|
| Exercise | Sets | Reps | Lbs |
| Overhead Dumbbell Presses | 2-3 | 12-15 | # |
|  |  |  |  |
|  |  |  |  |
|  |  |  |  |
|  |  |  |  |
|  |  |  |  |

# Close Reverse Grip Pull-Downs
## emphasis on the bicep and shoulders

a.  Sit in machine with upper-thigh wedged under pad to hold the body in  place.

b.  Your grip is 4-6 inches apart with palms facing you on bar.

c.  Inhale as you  pull toward collarbone

d.  Lean back  slightly, keeping the elbows in line with your wrists

e.  Exhale  as you extend arms upward, allowing your back muscles to  stretch at top of motion.

| Beginner-Upper Body Exercise | Sets | Reps | Lbs |
|---|---|---|---|
| Close reverse Pull-Downs | 2-3 | 12-15 | # |
|  |  |  |  |
|  |  |  |  |
|  |  |  |  |
|  |  |  |  |
|  |  |  |  |

# Crunches:
# abs of course!

a. Lie flat on your back.

b. Knees bent, feet flat on the floor about hip-distance apart.

c. Tilt your tailbone up toward the ceiling which will push your lower back into the floor. This is called a **pelvic tilt.**

d. Inhale and tighten abs by pulling the bellybutton toward the spine.

e. As you exhale, lift head, neck, and shoulders until u feel resistance, leading with the chest (keep shoulder blades drawn together)

NOTE: abs should be engaged throughout the entire movement. Do not release your contraction until the completion of the set.

**Beginner-Upper Body**

| Exercise | Sets | Reps | Lbs |
|---|---|---|---|
| Crunches | 2-3 | 15-20 | Self |
|  |  |  |  |
|  |  |  |  |
|  |  |  |  |
|  |  |  |  |
|  |  |  |  |

# Notes

| Beginner- Lower Body | | | |
| Exercise | Sets | Reps | Lbs |
|---|---|---|---|
| Leg Extension | 2-3 | 12-15 | # |
| Stationary Lunge | 2-3 | 10-12 each leg | Self |
| Lying Hamstring Curl | 2-3 | 10-12 | # |
| Standing Calf Raise | 2-3 | 15-20 | # |
| | | | |
| | | | |

# Leg Extension
## quadriceps (front of thighs)

a.  Adjust machine for your height.

b.  Sit in the machine, holding onto handles on either side of the seat to stabilize your body throughout the movement.

c.  Bend your knees and place ankles behind leg extension pads.

d.  Inhale while raising legs until they are parallel to the floor or until leg is straight.

e.  As u lower the weight, do not allow weight stack to touch. Focus on keeping the pressure on the quads.

| Beginner- Lower Body | | | |
|---|---|---|---|
| Exercise | Sets | Reps | Lbs |
| Leg Extension | 2-3 | 12-15 | # |
| | | | |
| | | | |
| | | | |
| | | | |
| | | | |

# Stationary Lunge
## entire lower body

a.  Place hands on hips with feet shoulder-width apart.

b.  With lunging leg, step forward either onto the floor or an elevation 3-5 inches high.

c.  Your lunging distance should be far enough so that you make a 90 degree angle with your working knee.

d.  Keep the upper body perpendicular to the floor.

e.  To return to starting position, push off with heel, bringing working leg back to starting position.

f.  Repeat reps on same leg.

g.  Switch legs and repeat.

| Beginner- Lower Body | | | |
|---|---|---|---|
| **Exercise** | **Sets** | **Reps** | **Lbs** |
| Stationary Lunge | 2-3 | 10-12 each leg | Self |
| | | | |
| | | | |
| | | | |
| | | | |
| | | | |

# Lying Hamstring Curl
## hamstrings, calves

a. Adjust machine so that pad rests on the Achilles tendon, right above the heel as you lie face down.

b. Inhale, curling the leg toward your butt, contracting the **hamstrings** completely.

c. Exhale as you straighten legs down.  Do not extend leg fully, keeping a slight bend in the knee.

| Beginner- Lower Body | | | |
|---|---|---|---|
| **Exercise** | **Sets** | **Reps** | **Lbs** |
| Lying Hamstring Curl | 2-3 | 10-12 | # |
|  |  |  |  |
|  |  |  |  |
|  |  |  |  |
|  |  |  |  |
|  |  |  |  |

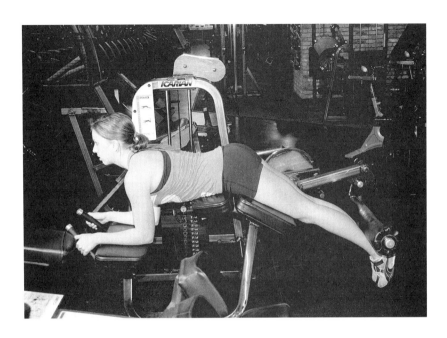

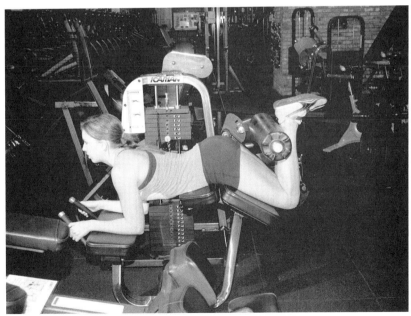

# Standing Calf Raises
## calves

a. Maintain balance, i.e., hold onto something and place one foot on the platform. Cross non-working leg behind the other.

b. With working leg, keep the ball of your foot on the platform with your heel hanging off.

c. Lower your heel toward the floor, stretching the calf with knee straight (knee is "locked out").

d. Reach a tip-toe position, rotating to the inner ball of the foot.

e. Contract the calf muscle, hold for one second, and return to starting position.

Complete reps and switch legs.

| Beginner- Lower Body | | | |
|---|---|---|---|
| **Exercise** | **Sets** | **Reps** | **Lbs** |
| Standing Calf Raise | 2-3 | 15-20 | # |
| | | | |
| | | | |
| | | | |
| | | | |
| | | | |

# Notes

| Intermediate- Upper Body | | | |
|---|---|---|---|
| Exercise | Sets | Reps | Lbs |
| Side Delt Raises | 3-4 | 12-15 | # |
| Dumbbell Presses | 3-4 | 12-15 | # |
| Wide Grip Pull-Downs | 3-4 | 12-15 | # |
| Incline Dumbbell Flyes | 3-4 | 15-20 | Self |
| Knee-Ups | 3-4 | 15-20 | Self |
|  |  |  |  |

# Side Delt Raises
## shoulders

a. Starting position: arms at the side, elbows slightly bent, palms facing the hips. Your feet are close together, knees slightly bent, back straight.

b. Raise arms laterally without bending your elbow until it is level with the shoulders.

c. Return to starting position and repeat

| Intermediate- Upper Body | | | |
|---|---|---|---|
| **Exercise** | **Sets** | **Reps** | **Lbs** |
| Side Delt Raises | 3-4 | 12-15 | # |
| | | | |
| | | | |
| | | | |
| | | | |
| | | | |

# Dumbbell Presses
## chest, shoulders, triceps

a.  Lie flat on the bench with your feet wider than your shoulders placed on the floor for stability.

b.  Extend your arms holding the dumbbells upward away from the body.  As you bring them down, keep them in the same plane as the middle of your chest.

c.  Lower the dumbbells so that you square up with your chest at the bottom of the motion. (The inside of the dumbbell should be at the outside of your chest at the bottom).

d.  As you press them back up in the same plane, (in line with the middle of your chest) exhale as you reach the top.

| Intermediate- Upper Body | | | |
| Exercise | Sets | Reps | Lbs |
| --- | --- | --- | --- |
| Dumbbell Presses | 3-4 | 12-15 | # |
| | | | |
| | | | |
| | | | |
| | | | |
| | | | |

# Wide Grip Pull-Downs
## upper back

a.  Take a wider than shoulder-width overhand grip on the bar.  Sit in the machine and lean slightly back, looking up at the pulley.

b.  Pull the bar toward the collarbone keeping your elbows back and wide, in line with the wrists.

c.  As you pull the bar down to your chest, inhale.

d.  As you extend your arms back up, exhale.

| Intermediate- Upper Body Exercise | Sets | Reps | Lbs |
|---|---|---|---|
| Wide Grip Pull-Downs | 3-4 | 12-15 | # |
|  |  |  |  |
|  |  |  |  |
|  |  |  |  |
|  |  |  |  |
|  |  |  |  |

# Incline Dumbbell Flyes
## upper chest, front of the shoulders

a. Lie on an inclined bench holding dumbbells together with your palms facing each other.

b. As you lower the dumbbells, inhale, maintaining a slight bend in your elbows.

c. Lower the dumbbells to the level of your upper chest and return exhaling, to the starting position without changing the angle of the elbows.

| Intermediate- Upper Body | | | |
|---|---|---|---|
| Exercise | Sets | Reps | Lbs |
| Incline Dumbbell Flyes | 3-4 | 15-20 | Self |
| | | | |
| | | | |
| | | | |
| | | | |
| | | | |

# Knee-Ups
## abs, hip flexors

a. Place your back flat on the pad and rest your elbows on the elbow support pads.

b. As you raise your knees, maintain a 90 degree angle with your legs. (Do not tuck your feet underneath your legs as you raise your knees).

c. Round your back so that you fully contract your abs. Exhale as you pull up, inhale as you lower your legs.

*Advanced version: Perform the movement with your legs straight*

| Intermediate- Upper Body | | | |
|---|---|---|---|
| **Exercise** | **Sets** | **Reps** | **Lbs** |
| Knee-Ups | 3-4 | 15-20 | Self |
| | | | |
| | | | |
| | | | |
| | | | |
| | | | |

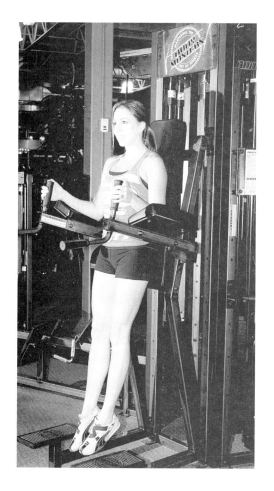

# Notes

| Intermediate- Lower body | | | |
|---|---|---|---|
| Exercise | Sets | Reps | Lbs |
| Alternating Walking Lunges | 3-4 | 12-15 | # |
| Leg Press (feet 10-12 inches apart) | 3-4 | 12-15 | # |
| Dumbbell Plie Squats | 3-4 | 12-15 | # |
| Dumbbell Stiff-Legged Deadlift | 3-4 | 12-15 | # |
| Standing Calf Raises | 3-4 | 12-15 | # |
|  |  |  |  |

# Alternating Walking Lunges
## entire lower body.

**NOTE:** It can be used with either dumbbells or a barbell for added resistance.

a.  Stand with your feet hip-shoulder width apart with hands on your hips. (If dumbbells are used, keep them next to your hips and do not swing them. If a barbell is used, place it across your shoulders).

b.  Keeping your torso as upright as possible, take a step forward with one leg, keeping it in line with its starting position.

c.  As you lunge for ward and kneel down, your front leg and torso should be at a 90 degree angle. Make sure your knee does not extend over your toes.

Next Page

| Intermediate- Lower body | | | |
|---|---|---|---|
| **Exercise** | **Sets** | **Reps** | **Lbs** |
| Alternating Walking Lunges | 3-4 | 12-15 | # |
| | | | |
| | | | |
| | | | |
| | | | |

d. Come up.  As you draw the other leg forward, bring your feet back to the starting position.

e. Alternate the move to the other leg.

# Leg Press
# thighs, rear

a. Place feet 10-12 inches apart in the center of the platform. Make sure your back is flat on the pad and lower the platform until your knees are at a 90 degree angle.

b. Keeping your feet flat on the platform, drive most of the pressure through your heels.

c. Extend your legs to the top of the movement where the knees are slightly bent. Do not lock your knees at the top of the movement.

| Exercise | Sets | Reps | Lbs |
|---|---|---|---|
| Leg Press (feet 10-12 inches apart) | 3-4 | 12-15 | # |
| | | | |
| | | | |
| | | | |
| | | | |
| | | | |

# Dumbbell Plie Squats
## entire lower body and especially inner thighs and rear

a. Feet are placed wider than shoulder-width apart with the toes pointing outward.

b. Squat down until your upper thighs are parallel with the ground.

c. Make a square with your legs at the bottom of the range of motion.

**Intermediate- Lower body**

| Exercise | Sets | Reps | Lbs |
|---|---|---|---|
| Dumbbell Plie Squats | 3-4 | 12-15 | # |
| | | | |
| | | | |
| | | | |
| | | | |
| | | | |

# Dumbbell Stiff-Legged Deadlift
# hamstrings, lower back.

a.  Start with feet hip-shoulder-width apart and parallel. Bend forward at the waist, keeping your back flat with eyes forward like an oriental bow.

b.  Lower the dumbbells toward your ankles. Keep your knees slightly bent.

c.  Return to starting position without changing the slight angle in the knee.

| Exercise | Sets | Reps | Lbs |
|---|---|---|---|
| Dumbbell Stiff-Legged | 3-4 | 12-15 | # |
|  |  |  |  |
|  |  |  |  |
|  |  |  |  |
|  |  |  |  |

# Standing Calf Raises
## calves

a. Maintain balance, i.e., hold onto something and place one foot on the platform. Cross non-working leg behind the other.

b. With working leg, keep the ball of your foot on the platform with your heel hanging off.

c. Lower your heel toward the floor, stretching the calf with knee straight (knee is "locked out").

d. Reach a tip-toe position, rotating to the inner ball of the foot.

e. Contract the calf muscle, hold for one second, and return to starting position.

f. Complete reps and switch legs.

| Intermediate- Lower body | | | |
|---|---|---|---|
| **Exercise** | **Sets** | **Reps** | **Lbs** |
| Standing Calf Raises | 3-4 | 12-15 | # |
| | | | |
| | | | |
| | | | |
| | | | |
| | | | |

# Notes

| Intermediate- Upper Body | | | |
|---|---|---|---|
| Exercise | Sets | Reps | Lbs |
| Dumbbell Rear Delt Flyes | 3-4 | 12-15 | # |
| Incline Dumbbell Presses | 3-4 | 12-15 | # |
| Cable Rows | 3-4 | 12-15 | # |
| Overhead Dumbbell Presses | 3-4 | 12-15 | # |
| Inclined Push-Ups | 3-4 | 12-15 | Self |
| Crunches | 3-4 | 20-30 | Self |

# Dumbbell Rear Delt Flye
# back of the shoulders, upper back

a. While holding dumbbells, stand with feet shoulder-width apart.

b. Bend knees slightly, then bend at the waist keeping back flat.

c. Position upper body so that your shoulders are slightly higher than your hips.

d. Face palms together and look straight ahead.

e. Raise arms laterally toward ceiling with elbows slightly bent.

f. Focus on squeezing shoulder blades together at the top of the movement.

g. At top, dumbbells should be parallel with the floor.

*Return dumbbells to starting position.*

| Intermediate- Upper Body | | | |
|---|---|---|---|
| Exercise | Sets | Reps | Lbs |
| Dumbbell Rear Delt Flyes | 3-4 | 12-15 | # |
| | | | |
| | | | |
| | | | |
| | | | |
| | | | |

# Incline Dumbbell Presses
## chest, shoulders, triceps
### (almost identical to regular dumbbell presses)

a. Lie flat on an inclined bench with your feet wider than your shoulders placed on the floor for stability.

b. Extend your arms holding the dumbbells upward away from the body.  As you bring them down, keep them in the same plane as the middle of your chest.

c. Lower the dumbbells so that you square up with your chest at the bottom of the motion.  (The inside of the dumbbell should be at the outside of your chest at the bottom).

d. As you press them back up in the same plane, (in line with the middle of your chest) exhale as you reach the top.

**Intermediate- Upper Body**

| Exercise | Sets | Reps | Lbs |
|---|---|---|---|
| Incline Dumbbell Presses | 3-4 | 12-15 | # |
|  |  |  |  |
|  |  |  |  |
|  |  |  |  |
|  |  |  |  |
|  |  |  |  |

# Cable Rows
## upper and lower back, rear delts, and biceps
### (Use the close-grip diamond bar for this movement)

a.  Sit in cable row machine with feet on stability platforms.

b.  Grab the bar with palms facing together.

c.  Bend at the waist with back flat (like rowing a boat), knees slightly bent.

d.  Lean forward 3-5 inches and inhale as you stretch lower back.

e.  Return to  upright position simultaneously pulling the bar to the abdomen. Concentrate on pulling with the elbows and squeezing shoulder blades together.

NOTE: Do not use rocking motion/momentum to aid in lifting the weight.  The movement should be fluid.2

| Intermediate- Upper Body | | | |
|---|---|---|---|
| **Exercise** | **Sets** | **Reps** | **Lbs** |
| Cable Rows | 3-4 | 12-15 | # |
| | | | |
| | | | |
| | | | |
| | | | |
| | | | |

# Overhead Dumbbell Presses
## shoulders and triceps (back of arms)

a.  Sit on utility bench.

b.  Lift dumbbells with palms facing forward, level with your ears.

c.  Keeping elbows in line/beneath the wrist, press dumbbells overhead, bringing them together at the top of the range of motion.

d.  As you bring them back down, stop at either ear level, or at a 90 degree angle at the elbow.

Note: This movement can also be performed with palms facing inward. This hits more of the front of your shoulder...

| Intermediate- Upper Body | | | |
|---|---|---|---|
| Exercise | Sets | Reps | Lbs |
| Overhead Dumbbell Presses | 3-4 | 12-15 | # |
| | | | |
| | | | |
| | | | |
| | | | |
| | | | |

# Inclined Push-Up
## chest, shoulders, triceps, core muscles

This is identical to a floor push-up. It allows a woman to go through the same range of motion with the added benefit of less resistance. This works the chest, deltoid (shoulder), triceps, and is an **isometric** contraction for the abs.

a. Place hands wider than shoulder-distance apart.

b. Adjust feet so that when u lower your upper body toward the bar, the mid-line of your chest touches the bar.

c. Keep elbows in line with the wrists.

d. Incorrect form is bringing your neck or clavicle toward the bar instead of your chest.

**Intermediate- Upper Body**

| Exercise | Sets | Reps | Lbs |
|---|---|---|---|
| Inclined Push-Ups | 3-4 | 12-15 | Self |
| | | | |
| | | | |
| | | | |
| | | | |
| | | | |

# Crunches:
# abs of course!

a. Lie flat on your back.

b. Knees bent, feet flat on the floor about hip-distance apart.

c. Tilt your tailbone up toward the ceiling which will push your lower back into the floor. This is called a **pelvic tilt.**

d. Inhale and tighten abs by pulling the bellybutton toward the spine.

e. As you exhale, lift head, neck, and shoulders until u feel resistance, leading with the chest (keep shoulder blades drawn together)

NOTE: Abs should be engaged throughout the entire movement. Do not release your contraction until the completion of the set.

| Intermediate- Upper Body | | | |
|---|---|---|---|
| Exercise | Sets | Reps | Lbs |
| Crunches | 3-4 | 20-30 | Self |
|  |  |  |  |
|  |  |  |  |
|  |  |  |  |
|  |  |  |  |
|  |  |  |  |

149

# Notes

| Advanced- Chest and Triceps | | | |
| --- | --- | --- | --- |
| **Exercise** | **Sets** | **Reps** | **Lbs** |
| Incline Dumbbell Presses | 4-5 | 12-15 | # |
| Regular Push-Ups | 5 sets or many as possible | 10-12 | Self |
| Bench Dips | 3-4 sets | 12-15 | Self |
| Overhead Tricep Extension with Cable | 3 | 15 | # |
| Tricep Pressdown | 3-4 | 12-15 | # |
| | | | |

# Incline Dumbbell Presses
## upper chest, front of the shoulders
### (almost identical to regular dumbbell presses)

a. Lie flat on an inclined bench with your feet wider than your shoulders placed on the floor for stability.

b. Extend your arms holding the dumbbells upward away from the body. As you bring them down, keep them in the same plane as the middle of your chest.

c. Lower the dumbbells so that you square up with your chest at the bottom of the motion. (The inside of the dumbbell should be at the outside of your chest at the bottom.)

d. As you press them back up in the same plane, (in line with the middle of your chest) exhale as you reach the top.

| Advanced- Chest and Triceps | | | |
|---|---|---|---|
| **Exercise** | **Sets** | **Reps** | **Lbs** |
| Incline Dumbbell Presses | 4-5 | 12-15 | # |
| | | | |
| | | | |
| | | | |
| | | | |
| | | | |

# Regular Push-Ups
## chest, shoulders, triceps, and core muscles

a. Position yourself in push-up position on the floor so your hands are wider than shoulder-distance apart and your chest is above and in line with your hands.

b. Lower your body so that you hit a 90 degree angle or less at your elbows, bringing your chest between your hands.

c. Keep your body straight throughout the range of motion and return to starting position.

| Advanced- Chest and Triceps | | | |
|---|---|---|---|
| **Exercise** | **Sets** | **Reps** | **Lbs** |
| Regular Push-Ups | 5 sets (or many as possible) | 10-12 | Self |
| | | | |
| | | | |
| | | | |
| | | | |
| | | | |

# Bench Dips
## chest, shoulder, triceps

a. Sit on the edge of a bench, placing palms next to your hips, gripping the bench's edge.

b. Place feet together flat on the floor 2-3 feet away from the bench.

c. Slide off of the bench, keeping your body 1-2 inches away from the edge.

d. Bend at the elbows, lowering your body so that you hit a 90 degree angle (shoulder level with the elbows).

e. Return to starting position, keeping hips directly beneath the shoulders.

Note: To increase difficulty level, perform movement with legs straight.

| Advanced- Chest and Triceps | | | |
|---|---|---|---|
| **Exercise** | **Sets** | **Reps** | **Lbs** |
| Bench Dips | 3-4 sets | 12-15 | Self |
| | | | |
| | | | |
| | | | |
| | | | |
| | | | |

# Overhead Tricep Extension With Cable
## triceps and core

**NOTE:** This exercise can be performed with the rope, straight or cambered (bent)bar. If applicable, adjust the height of the pulley so that it's above your head.

a. Back up to the machine and place hands on grips.

b. Put your feet close together with knees bent.

c. Bend at your waist, keeping your shoulders slightly higher than your hips.

d. Extend hands out, keeping elbows level with your ears.

e. Bend at the elbows, bringing the hands behind the head and extend back to starting position.

| Advanced- Chest and Triceps | | | |
|---|---|---|---|
| **Exercise** | **Sets** | **Reps** | **Lbs** |
| Overhead tricep extension with cable | 3 | 15 | # |
| | | | |
| | | | |
| | | | |
| | | | |
| | | | |

# Tricep Pressdown with Cambered Bar
## triceps

a. Attach a cambered bar to a high-pulley cable. With your knees slightly bent, lean forward a bit at the waist and pin your elbows to your sides as you bring your lower arms just above parallel to the floor.

b. Look forward, keeping your torso erect and your abs tight.

c. Flex your triceps and press the handle toward the floor until your arms are fully extended. Squeeze your tris and hold for a brief count before returning to the start position.

**Advanced- Chest and Triceps**

| Exercise | Sets | Reps | Lbs |
|---|---|---|---|
| Tricep Pressdown | 3-4 | 12-15 | # |
| | | | |
| | | | |
| | | | |
| | | | |
| | | | |

# Notes

| Advanced-Legs Exercise | Sets | Reps | Lbs |
|---|---|---|---|
| Barbell Squat | 4-5 | 12-15 | # |
| Leg Press | 3-4 | 12-15 | # |
| Walking Lunges with Dumbbells | 2-3 | 12-15 | 8-15 |
| Lying Hamstring Curls | 2-3 | 12-15 | # |
|  |  |  |  |
|  |  |  |  |

# Barbell Squat
## entire lower body

a. Walk into squat rack, place hands equal distance apart on the bar.

b. As you cross under the bar, and place it on your shoulders, make sure it is centered and balanced.

c. Place feet parallel and slightly wider than shoulder-distance apart.

d. Set your hips back and down like you're sitting in a chair until the top of your thigh is parallel to the ground.

| Advanced-Legs Exercise | Sets | Reps | Lbs |
|---|---|---|---|
| Barbell Squat | 4-5 | 12-15 | # |
| | | | |
| | | | |
| | | | |
| | | | |
| | | | |

e.  Throughout range of motion, keep feet flat on the floor, with 80% of the pressure in your heels.

f.  Remember to lean slightly forward with upper body to maintain balance and return to starting position

# Leg Press
## thigh, rear

a. Place feet 10-12 inches apart in the center of the platform. Make sure your back is flat on the pad and lower the platform until your knees are at a 90 degree angle.

b. Keeping your feet flat on the platform, drive most of the pressure through your heels.

c. Extend your legs to the top of the movement where the knees are slightly bent. Do not lock your knees at the top of the movement.

| Advanced-Legs Exercise | Sets | Reps | Lbs |
|---|---|---|---|
| Leg Press | 3-4 | 12-15 | # |
|  |  |  |  |
|  |  |  |  |
|  |  |  |  |
|  |  |  |  |
|  |  |  |  |

# Walking Lunges with Dumbells
## entire lower body

a. Stand with feet shoulder-width apart, holding the dumbbells down at your side.

b. Keeping your torso upright, step forward with one leg. As you bend your front knee, drop your back knee toward the floor without letting it touch. Push up through your front heel, straightening your leg.

c. Bring your leg forward and past the opposite leg to take the next step, making sure your knee doesn't pass your toes in the bottom position.

d. Repeat for reps, alternating legs to move forward.

| Advanced-Legs Exercise | Sets | Reps | Lbs |
|---|---|---|---|
| Walking Lunges with Dumbbells | 2-3 | 12-15 | 8-15 |
| | | | |
| | | | |
| | | | |
| | | | |
| | | | |

# Lying Hamstring Curl
## hamstrings, calves

a. Adjust machine so that pad rests on the Achilles tendon, right above the heel as you lie face down.

b. Inhale, curling the leg toward your butt, contracting the hamstrings completely

c. Exhale as you straighten legs down. Do not extend leg fully, keeping a slight bend in the knee.

| Advanced-Legs Exercise | Sets | Reps | Lbs |
|---|---|---|---|
| Lying Hamstring Curls | 2-3 | 12-15 | # |
|  |  |  |  |
|  |  |  |  |
|  |  |  |  |
|  |  |  |  |
|  |  |  |  |

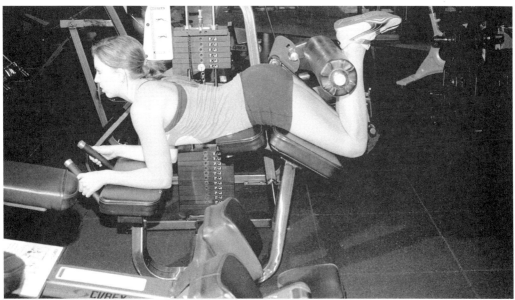

# Notes

| Advanced-Back and Biceps Exercise | Sets | Reps | Lbs |
|---|---|---|---|
| Close reverse grip pull downs | 4-5 | 12-15 | # |
| Barbell Row | 3-4 | 12-15 | # |
| Wide Grip Pull- Downs | 3 | 12-15 | # |
| Alternating Dumbbell Curls | 3 | 15-20 | # |
| | | | |
| | | | |

# Close Reverse Grip Pull-Downs
## total back with emphasis on the bicep and shoulders

a. Sit in machine with upper-thigh wedged under pad to hold the body in place.

b. Your grip is 4-6 inches apart with palms facing you on bar.

c. Inhale as you pull toward collarbone

d. Lean back slightly, keeping the elbows in line with your wrists.

e. Exhale as you extend arms upward, allowing your back muscles to stretch at top of motion.

| Advanced-Back and Biceps | | | |
|---|---|---|---|
| Exercise | Sets | Reps | Lbs |
| Close reverse grip pull downs | 4-5 | 12-15 | # |
| | | | |
| | | | |
| | | | |
| | | | |
| | | | |

# Barbell Rows
# back and biceps

a. Hold the barbell with an overhand or underhand grip wider than shoulder distance apart.

b. Keeping your back flat, bend slightly at the knees and lean forward positioning your upper body almost parallel to the ground with your shoulders slightly higher than your hips.

c. In a rowing motion, keep your elbows in line with your wrists while pulling towards the middle of your torso and back down.

| Advanced-Back and Biceps | | | |
|---|---|---|---|
| Exercise | Sets | Reps | Lbs |
| Barbell Row | 3-4 | 12-15 | # |
| | | | |
| | | | |
| | | | |
| | | | |
| | | | |

# Wide Grip Pull-Downs
## upper back

a.  Take a wider than shoulder-width overhand grip on the bar.  Sit in the machine and lean slightly back, looking up at the pulley.

b.  Pull the bar toward  the collarbone keeping your elbows back and wide, in line with the wrists.

c.  As you pull the bar down to your chest, inhale.

d.  As you extend your arms back up, exhale.

| Exercise | Sets | Reps | Lbs |
|---|---|---|---|
| Wide Grip Pull- Downs | 3 | 12-15 | # |
|  |  |  |  |
|  |  |  |  |
|  |  |  |  |
|  |  |  |  |
|  |  |  |  |

# Alternating Dumbbell Curls
# biceps

**NOTE:** This exercise can be done in either the seated or standing position.

a. If standing, place feet about shoulder width apart and bend slightly at the knees.

b. Holding the dumbbells in each hand, keep the shoulders and the elbows back in line with your torso.

c. Curl one arm at a time, bringing your wrist toward your shoulder then back to starting position with your wrist facing your hips

**Advanced-Back and Biceps**

| Exercise | Sets | Reps | Lbs |
|---|---|---|---|
| Alternating Dumbbell Curls | 3 | 15-20 | # |
| | | | |
| | | | |
| | | | |
| | | | |
| | | | |

# Notes

# Appendix 3

# Miss University F.Y.I.'s

**FYI-1**   Cindy Maynard, M.S., R.D., "Dying to Fit In- Literally!" Learning to Love Our Bodies and Ourselves," Eating Disorder Reference and Information Center, http://www.edreferral.com/body (accessed July 18, 2007).

**FYI-2**   Alice Covey, C.D., R.D., "Dieting as a Precursor to Eating Disorders," Eating Disorder Reference and Information Center http:://edreferral.com/Articles/ (accessed July 18, 2007).

**FYI-3**   CNN.com,http://cnn.com/HEALTH/library/HQ/01710.html accessed July 18, 2007).

**FYI-4**   Media Awareness Network,"Beauty and Body Image in the Media" http://www.mediaawareness.ca/english/issues/stereotyping/women_and_g irls/women_beauty.cfm (accessed July 18, 2007).

**FYI-5**   Mayoclinic.com, http://www.mayoclinic.com/health/aerobic-exercise/EP00002. (accessed July 18, 2007).

**FYI-6**   Barbara Russi Sarnataro,"The Basics: Build Muscle for Better Health" Webmd.com, http://www.webmd.com/fitness-exercise/features/. (accessed July 20, 2007).

**FYI-7**   Mayoclinic.com, http://www.mayoclinic.com/health/food-and-nutrition/NU00197. (accessed July 18, 2007).

**FYI-8**   Mayoclinic.com, /HQ01396 (accessed July 18, 2007). http://www.mayoclinic.com/health/healthydiet

**FYI-9**   Webmd.com,http://www.webmd.com/a-to-z- guides/features/
power-nap?page=2
(accessed July 18, 2007).

**FYI-10**  Webmd.com,
http://www.webmd.com/osteoporosis/how-much-calcium. (accessed July
20, 2007).

**FYI-11**  Webmd.com,http://www.webmd.com/fitnessexercise/benefits-of-
exercise (accessed July 20, 2007).

# Glossary

# Glossary

**Aerobics**-Used to define classes that combine endurance and toning exercises over a prolonged period of time (30-60 minutes). Aerobics classes include numerous activities to increase the heart and respiratory rate. Some examples include dance-based aerobics class; step aerobics; fusion aerobics, which combine 2-3 types of classes; and basic training/boot-camp classes.

**Amino Acids**- The chemical (molecular) substances that make up protein. They are simply the building blocks of protein. Protein broken down in the digestive system (amino acids) are used for repairing muscle tissue as well as organs, skin, bone, hair, and nails.

**Body Composition**-Your composition is the breakdown of the percentages of body fat, fat-free mass (FFM), total body water (TBW), and basal metabolic rate (BMR). Having this knowledge makes it much easier to be more accurate with the diet and exercise regime.

**Carbohydrates**- Based upon their chemical structure, carbohydrates are categorized into either simple of complex. Both, like protein, have four calories per gram and are also digested into blood sugar called glucose. With the help of insulin, the glucose is then stored in the form of *glycogen* in our muscles and liver with the excess being stored as fat and used to circulate blood glucose. *Simple carbohydrates* are rapidly digested. Many simply carbohydrates contain processed sugars and are low in essential vitamins and minerals. Examples include soft drinks, cookies, candy, chocolate, syrup, and of course, sugar. *Complex carbohydrates* take longer to digest and are generally more nutritious as they contain more vitamins, minerals, and fiber.  Examples are potatoes, oatmeal, legumes,whole grain breads and pasta.

**Cardio Threshold**- Also referred to as the *lactic acid* or *anaerobic threshold.* It is the point when lactic acid starts to accumulate in the muscles, and is considered to be between 85 and 90 percent of your maximum heart rate. This is approximately 40 beats higher than the *aerobic threshold*, which is measured by the point at which anaerobic energy sequences begin to operate, and is considered to be around 65 percent of maximum heart rate. Conversely, the anaerobic threshold is considered to be 40 beats lower than the lactic acid threshold.

**Catabolic State**- Considered the muscle wasting/losing state.  If you are on a very low calorie diet (VLCD), in the absence of glycogen and amino acids for energy, the body will break down muscle tissue in the form of amino acids to use for energy. The best way to deter this state is to get enough rest and eat small frequent meals containing both protein and carbohydrates.

**Circuit Boxing**- This is a total body cardiovascular workout that focuses on muscle conditioning with varying exercise stations. These classes typically utilize boxing and kicking techniques on different types of punching bags during timed intervals alternating with rest periods.

**Dehydration**- is a result of excessive fluid loss from the body.

Dehydration is brought on by evaporation, perspiration, urination, and fever. If you do not drink enough fluid, it can lower your metabolism as well as your fat burning potential.

**Fat Free Mass** (FFM)- consists of muscle, skin, organs, bone, hair, nails, etc. It is everything that is not fat. Your FFM is comprised of 50-60% water.

**Glycogen**- Simply put, it is the stored form of glucose (sugar). Our bodies store excess carbohydrates as glycogen in the muscles and the liver, or as fat. In a glycogen depleted state, the body turns to its protein (muscle) sources for energy.

**Hypoglycemia**- referred to as low blood sugar that results in a feeling of anxiety, cold sweats, dizziness, and feeling light-headed. If this occurs, stop your workout and drink a sports drink like Gatorade that is high in sugar to get your blood sugar levels closer to normal. Eat a meal containing protein and carbohydrates soon after.

**Kickboxing**- a high impact cardiovascular workout that combines elements of aerobics, boxing, and martial arts into a 30-60 minute exercise routine. This is a lot of fun, and with an experienced instructor, it can be done at the beginner level all the way up to advanced. Cardio-kickboxing burns an average of 350-450 calories per hour.

**Metabolism**- Is the combination of anabolism and catabolism. Anabolism is the synthesis, or building, of organic molecules. Catabolism is the breakdown (digestion/absorption) of these substances.

**Post Workout Meal**- next to breakfast, it is one of the two most important meals of the day. It is very important to eat a balanced meal, complete with protein and complex carbohydrates, so your body is able to replenish the muscle and liver glycogen stores as well as the protein (amino acids) necessary for rebuilding and repairing the damaged tissues. Also, this keeps the body from breaking down current muscles for amino acids.

**Skin Fold Caliper Test**- like the body composition analysis/scale, this is very popular among most gyms and professional trainers for finding out your body composition. It is simply several measurements in various areas of the body, which are different between males and females. Once these measurements are added up, there are charts available to give you your fat percentage with approximately a **+/-** 3% variance.

**Spinning**- a low-high intensity stationary cycling class that involves interval training. Spin classes are one of the fastest ways to tone your lower body. It's also extremely beneficial to your cardiovascular system.

# WITHDRAWN

## DATE DUE

| | | | |
|---|---|---|---|
| | | | |
| | | | |
| | | | |
| | | | |
| | | | |
| | | | |
| | | | |
| | | | |
| | | | |
| | | | |
| | | | |
| | | | |
| | | | |
| | | | |
| | | | |
| | | | |
| | | | |
| | | | |
| | | | |